For Tucker

David Johnson

DEDICATION

I was blessed to have some great teachers who, in their own ways, helped me to become the writer I am today. I'm indebted to them all!

- Mrs. Julia Rich, my high school 11th grade English teacher. She taught me how to conjugate verbs and to think for myself.

- Mrs. V.J. Shanklin, my high school 12th grade English teacher. She taught me the importance of good punctuation.

- Dr. Porter King, who taught my English Literature classes in my Freshmen and Sophomore college years. He helped me understand form and simplicity in writing.

- Author Sylvie Kurtz, who was my instructor a few years ago when I took a course in creative writing from the Long Ridge Writing School. She showed me how to make my stories feel more immediate and how to make the reader feel they are in the story.

ACKNOWLEDGMENTS

It is all the fans of <u>Tucker's Way</u>, and their clamoring to know more about Tucker and her story, that pushed me to complete this second book in the series. It's all of your all's positive comments that gave me the confidence that I needed to continue Tucker's story. I sincerely appreciate every one of you!

Chapter One

Shading his eyes from the brilliant sun, Smiley Carter enjoys the beauty of the cloudless, turquoise-colored, February sky. His almond-colored palms compliment the dark, coffee-colored skin of his face. Ivory-colored teeth fill his smile as his thick lips part. White eyebrows sit like snow-capped mountains above his dark eyes.

He steers his Ford 801 tractor into Tucker's front yard. As it rolls to a stop, he reduces the throttle and cuts off the engine.

Raising a gloved hand, he hollers, "Hello Tucker!"

The seat squeaks as he lifts his large frame and steps to the ground.

Joining him, Tucker looks up and says, "How y' been Smiley Carter? Ain't seen y' 'round in a while."

Taking off his cap to reveal white, close-cropped hair, Carter slaps Tucker on the shoulder. "Ol' lady Tucker. Hows you been? You know ol' Smiley Carter is one busy man."

Tucker rocks a step. Recovering her balance, she says, "One o' these days you're gonna call me that and I'm gonna knock them iv'ry teeth out, y' smilin' fool."

Carter bends double as a hearty laugh escapes him. "Now you knows you ain't gonna hurt ol' Smiley Carter. Cause if y' does, whose gonna plow your garden for y'?"

One corner of Tucker's mouth turns up imperceptibly and then retreats. "I ain't worried. I know yore granny, Mama Mattie, made y' promise to help me whenever I needed it."

Nodding somberly, Carter says, "'Tis so, 'tis so. An' if'n I don't, I'm afeered she'll come back and haunt me."

Tucker slaps him hard on the back. Carter stumbles forward.

Smiling, she says, "So y'ain't got no way outta it. Foller me 'n see what I need y' t' do."

Straightening up, Carter arches his back. As Tucker walks away he says, "Damn woman. I think you done broke somethin' in my back."

Carter catches up with her halfway to her barn. As he comes even with her, she says, "I'm ready t' plant m' early garden."

"You always does that in Februrary, doesn't you?" Carter asks.

"That's cause there's always one week in th' month that th' ground gits dry enough to plow," Tucker replies. "Irish taters, green peas, n' carrots all does better th' earlier you can get'em in th' ground."

"You plantin' in the same place as usual?" Carter asks.

"Naw. I moved th' hogs t' th' other side o' th' barn, into th' ol' garden spot. I wantchu t' plow up th' ol' pen area. It oughta be good n' rich."

Lifting the latch on the double barn door, Tucker swings them wide. Sunlight cascades into the dark hallway. Sitting in a circle around a large tub are March, August, April, Maisy and Ella. They turn toward the brilliant sun and the silhouetted pair in the door way. Their faces look as if like they've been hit with a spotlight.

Not until he speaks does anyone recognize Tucker's partner. "Hello chill'uns," Carter calls out.

Jumping to his feet, March exclaims, "Smiley Carter!" and runs to greet him.

Carter catches the boy, as he leaps toward him, and swings him skyward. "My goodness March! You have grown, boy."

August is on March's heels, but slows to a stop when he gets to Carter. "Hey Smiley Carter," he says.

Dropping March to the ground, Carter turns his attention to August. He begins walking around August, shaking his head. "And who is this tall, strappin' boy? Tucker, you used to have a skinny kid hangin' 'round here. What happened to him?"

Unable to contain himself, August says, "It's me. I'm that boy."

Carter crouches into a boxer's stance and starts throwing air punches toward August. "Let's see if you is. The boy I remember had lightning fast hands."

August responds by assuming a mirroring stance. He steps toward Carter and throws five quick punches to Carter's mid-section. Bouncing backward, he thumbs his nose and blows air out of it.

Carter collapses to the ground howling. "Tucker! It's my liver! That boy done ruptured my liver!"

August runs quickly to Carter's side and falls to his knees. "I'm sorry. I didn't mean nothing by it. I just meant to be playing with you."

Quick as a flash, Carter bear hugs August and rolls across the ground, laughing loudly. He stops rolling and pins August on his back. "Don't you worry about ol' Smiley Carter. I can still manage to take care of myself against any young pup like you."

Smiling, Carter gets off the ground and offers a hand to August. August grabs the hand and Carter pulls him into a warm embrace.

In the meantime, Ella, April and Maisy have gathered round to witness the commotion.

Spying April, Carter squats in front of her but still has to drop his head to look her in the eye. "And here's beautiful April, as pretty as the dogwoods in spring. Have you decided to talk to ol' Smiley Carter yet?"

3

April looks toward Ella. Ella nods. "Hi Smiley," April says softly.

Carter's eyes and mouth open wide. As if shoved backward by April, he falls on his rear. Looking at Tucker, he says, "What is this?" and points toward April.

"They's been some changes 'roun' 'ere since you was last 'ere. April's been a talkin' ever since Christmas."

Carter reaches slowly toward April. He touches her face, his large hand dwarfing her small features. "An' just like dogwoods bloom after a long winter, so has you chil'. So has you."

Placing her hands on her hips, Maisy says, "Well aren't you even going to speak to me? What's a woman have to do to get noticed, anyway?"

Getting off the ground and brushing himself off, Carter turns to look at Maisy. He coughs and spits. He gives her a curt, "Hello."

Turning toward Ella, he says, "Don't believe I ever met you ma'am."

Tucker speaks up. "That there's Miss Ella. She moved in t'th' McDaniel place a few months ago."

Flashing a broad smile, Carter bows to Ella and says, "Pleased to meet you Miss Ella. People 'round here calls me Smiley Carter."

Ella returns his smile and says, "Pleased to meet you Smiley Carter."

Stomping the ground, Maisy turns and heads back to the barn, muttering under her breath, "Well I never! 'Pleased to meet you Miss Ella.' You'd think she was the Queen of England or something."

Clapping his hands, Carter says, "Okay, let's get busy plowin' and a plantin'." He steps onto his tractor and fires up the hammering engine. He checks to be sure the twelve-inch two-bottom plow behind the tractor is off the ground and then follows Tucker's lead to the old hog pen.

"Which way you want the rows to run?" he hollers at Tucker over the sound of the engine.

"North and south," Tucker hollers back.

Carter backs the tractor into position, lowers the plow to the ground, shifts to first gear and heads south. The points of the plow slide easily into the nutrient-rich dirt, folding over the dark top soil in neat, humped rows behind the tractor. The smell of humus fills the air.

Looking at Carter's audience lined up along the fence, Tucker says, "Ya'll got them seed taters cut up and ready fer plantin?"

~~~~~~~~~~~~~~~~~~~~~~

Chapter Two

Making a sound like fabric tearing, the slicing of potatoes fills the silence in the barn hallway. The potato wedges fall one at a time into the waiting washtub. In order to avoid cutting a thumb or finger, everyone is focused on the task.

Tucker lifts her head as she hears Carter's tractor leaving the side of the barn and heading past the door.

Carter slows as he passes the entrance and calls out, "I'm going to get the disc. I'll be back in a bit."

Tucker waves without saying anything.

Maisy stands and wipes her hands on a rag she pulls from her back pocket. "Well I've got to be going."

"We ain't near done yet," Tucker growls.

"I know," Maisy says, "but I've got plans for the evening. I've got to get home and get cleaned up."

Tucker spits a stream of tobacco juice into the dirt floor of the barn. "Plans! I jes' wish I could live t' see th' day that you finish somethin' y' start. We've still gotta plant these taters. And I got some carrot seed, too."

Folding her arms across her chest, Maisy snaps, "I done more than my fair share when I was growin' up. You worked me like a dog when I was little – fetchin' water, choppin' kindling. It was never enough for you. Even when I said I was sick, I got the back of your hand and was told to get back to work."

Ella looks apprehensively toward Tucker.

Tucker slowly wipes her knife blade on her pants and stands up. In an even voice, she says, "You done?"

Maisy blinks and says, "Well, yes."

"Then git. Yain't no help 'ere anyways."

As Maisy retreats toward the house, Tucker says, "You kids help me lift this tub and take to the garden." Pointing toward a door, she adds, "Ella, look in there an' bring a couple o' hoes an' a rake."

When they all get to the garden site, the sound of Carter's approaching tractor is heard in the distance. In a moment he comes rolling through the gate, drops the disc behind him, and begins churning the thick upturned soil into fine powder.

"That is beautiful," Ella says to no one in particular. Kneeling down, she sinks her hands into the womb of the earth. "I've never been this close to this kind of thing. It's about rebirth and rejuvenation. And look at all these earthworms!"

August and March look at each other and shrug their shoulders.

"Bring me a hoe," Tucker says to March. "Bring some taters August."

Ella rises and walks toward Tucker.

Making his last pass over the garden spot, Carter lets the tractor roll to a stop and cuts off the engine. He gets stiffly off the tractor and joins everyone.

"Miss Ella," Carter says. "Did you wrap newspaper 'round those taters?"

Ella looks at the tub of potatoes and then to Tucker. "I....guess not......I just did like everyone else......"

"Then how you expect to keep that dirt outta their eyes?" Carter quizzes.

There is a pause and suddenly everyone except Ella bursts into laughter. Realizing she's been the brunt of a joke, Ella laughs, too.

"I remember when you got me on that one, Smiley Carter," August says.

"Don't think nothin' about it, Miss Ella," Carter laughs. "Smiley Carter's always pullin' somethin' on folks."

"No offense taken," Ella smiles.

Tucker digs into the soil with her hoe. "Ya'll quitcher carryin' on and drop a tater in this hole."

Moving quickly, August grabs a potato and drops it in. In three quick swipes with her hoe, Tucker buries the potato and tamps it. Without pausing, she moves one step and digs another hole. This time March drops a potato in.

"Yous plantin' too deep," Carter says. "They'll never sprout."

Without looking up, Tucker says, "Th' day Smiley Carter kin teach me somethin' 'bout growin' a garden is th' day.............is th' day Maisy does an honest day's work."

Carter laughs. "You would says that when you has a hoe in your hand, if you gets my meanin'."

Turning to Ella, he says, "Miss Ella, why don't you n' me shows them how to plant a garden?"

Knowing a covert message has just past between Carter and Tucker, Ella is a bit hesitant how to proceed. "I've never planted a garden before," she finally says.

"Well you's about to learn from the king," Carter boasts. "Take off your hat n' roll up your sleeves, cause Smiley Carter don't take no prisoners. Bring me that other hoe, April."

As April begins dragging the hoe toward Carter, Ella puts her hand on her hat.

"Quit bossin' people around, Smiley Carter," Tucker snaps. "She don't hav't' take off 'er hat if she don't wanna."

Carter stops and looks at Tucker, then to Ella. He notices Ella is blushing. "Sho' nuff that's so, Miss Ella. It don't matter. Just grab a double handful of taters and drop 'em in while I dig the hole." In Tucker's direction he adds, "And not too deep a hole, either."

He ducks just in time to miss a well-aimed dirt clog thrown by Tucker. August and March laugh loudly.

Feigning hurt, Carter says, "See hows they treats me 'round here Miss Ella? It ain't christian-like."

Soon they all settle into a steady rhythm of planting, August and March taking turns replenishing Ella's supply of potatoes.

After a few moments of quiet, Carter says to Ella, "You from around here? Don't believe I caught your last name."

Without glancing up, Ella says, "You might as well know, I'm the ex-wife of Judge Jack McDade. It sort of depends on how well a person knows him as to how a person feels about that. I think I'm prouder of being his ex than – "

She suddenly notices that Carter has dropped his hoe. Looking up, she sees him staring at her with his mouth agape.

"Did you say Judge Jack McDade?"

"Yes, that's right. Like I was saying, I think – "

"An' you's done made friends with Tucker?"

"Well, yes. I think we have become friends. Why?"

"'Cause this is a day to remember. Ol' Smiley Carter done seen him two miracles in the same day – April a talkin' and Tucker having as a friend the ex-wife of Judge Jack McDade. Yes sir, this here's a day to remember."

~~~~~~~~~~~~~~~~~~

Chapter Three

Sitting on the side of the bed, Maisy fumbles in the darkness for her cigarettes on the night stand. She extracts a cigarette and places it between her lips. Her zippo lighter clinks as she opens it and strikes a flame. Touching the flame to the end of her cigarette, she inhales deeply.

The flickering flame reveals smudged eye makeup. Her tangled dark hair gives her the semblance of Medusa.

She feels the bed move and hears a low groan. Smiling she says, "Hey Tiger. I thought you had gone into a coma. Was I too much for you?"

A male voice comes from under the covers. "Woman you're killing me."

Moving across the bed, Maisy straddles her partner. Pulling down the covers from his face, she enjoys the spreading smile on his face as he takes in her naked body.

"I still got it, don't I?" Maisy teases.

"What time is it?" he replies. "I've got to be going."

In a petulant voice, Maisy says, "'What time is it?' What kind of answer is that?! You wasn't in no hurry a while ago. I sometimes think you're just using me."

"Now Maisy, don't get all stirred up. You know how it is with me."

Unstraddling her quarry, Maisy reaches for her t-shirt and pulls it over her head, shaking out her curls as she does so. "I'm about sick of that line." In a mocking tone she adds, "'You know how it is with me.'"

Sitting up, he reaches for the lamp and switches it on. They both squint as their eyes adjust.

His red hair catches the light and frames his face in amber

hues. Fixing her with his clear, blue eyes he says, "You and I both know that I'm not the first guy you've danced with, so why should you think you've got sole possession of me?"

Maisy bursts into tears. "Are you calling me some kind of tramp or something? I've made mistakes in the past. I admit it. But it's different with you. I love you!"

She moves beside him. Putting her head on his chest and slipping her hand under the covers she says, "You know you want me."

Grabbing her arm, he pulls it out from under the covers. "Look, I've got to get ready for work."

He reaches for his pants on the floor and, standing, slips them on.

Maisy's voice gets a little louder. "Oh, so you think you're too good for me. Is that what it is? You think you can do better?"

Without looking in her direction he says, "I never said that, Maisy."

He walks to the bathroom and begins brushing his teeth. As he lifts his head from the sink to look in the mirror, a glass ashtray whistles past his ear. It hits the mirror. They both explode, sending shards of glass in a hundred directions.

Whirling around he finds Maisy standing ten feet away with her fists clinched and eyes wide.

"Are you crazy woman?! You could have killed me! What do you think you're doing?"

Maisy looks at him squarely. "You are not dumping me. Do you hear me? You are *not* dumping me."

Stepping carefully over the broken glass, he walks back into the room and picks up his shoes.

Maisy moves quickly to him. "Here let me help you," she

11

says sweetly. "I'm sorry. I didn't mean to scare you. I just lost my temper. Sit down. I'll put your shoes on you. Don't be mad at me."

Her hands tremble as she tries to slip his shoe on his foot.

Watching her sitting on her knees between his legs gives him pleasure. "How long have we been seeing each other Maisy?"

Maisy pauses. Thinking she hears a conciliatory tone, she slips closer to him. "It's been six years, three months and five days. We're meant for each other."

Taking his face in her hands, she purrs, "Let's go get in the shower."

"As much as I'd like to, I've got to go."

"Fine!" Maisy snaps. "Go ahead and leave. I don't care."

Picking his keys off the table, he heads out the door. As the door closes, he hears Maisy call out, "I love you Tiger!"

Moving to the window, Maisy watches him pull away from her apartment. Once he has driven out of sight, she goes to the phone. Dialing a number from memory, she waits for it to be answered.

In her cheeriest voice she says, "Hello Tom. What have you been up to? I haven't heard from you in a while. Why don't you drop by this afternoon and let's get reacquainted."

Meanwhile, as he drives away from Maisy's apartment, he begins an internal dialogue. *What am I going to do with that woman? I'll lose my wife, family and my job if anyone finds out about us.*

Me and Tucker's daughter! He laughs out loud at the implausibility of it.

How did I ever get involved with her?

His mind turns back to his first encounter with her at the Elk's Lodge. He spotted her dancing to Jerry Lee Lewis's "Chantilly Lace" playing on the juke box. Her dark hair bounced in rhythm to the music as her body skipped lithely across the floor. Her ample breasts moved to their own rhythm.

After the song, she walked to the bar and stood beside him, humming "Don't the Girls All Get Prettier at Closing Time." She turned to him and smiled. Her iridescent blue eyes made his heart stop. He was spellbound.

Chuckling, she'd said, "Like what you see?"

That's when he realized he'd been staring.

Quickly recovering, he said, "I sure do. Can I buy you a beer?"

"That'd be nice," she replied.

"What's your name?" he asked.

"Some people call me 'Amazing.' But I'll let you decide for yourself if that's what you want to call me."

At that point he really didn't care what her name was or where she was from. He wanted her.

That night they drove the twenty miles to the Blue Bank motel, a quiet place beside Reelfoot Lake. Later, he told her she was well deserving of the name "Amazing."

In the ensuing six years their relationship has been hot and cold. He's tried to sever ties with her, but there is something about her that he finds irresistible.

She's not the only woman he's seen through the years, but she is the one constant in his "stable" of women.

Today's attempt by her to hit him with the ashtray has left him shaken. Her behavior is more extreme and desperate each time he leaves her.

Maybe it's time for me to end things with her once and for all.

But how?

~~~~~~~~~~~~~~~~

Chapter Four

Tucker, August, and March sit silently eating supper. The only sounds are their forks on their plates and the cold, March wind whistling through the cracks around the doors and windows.

Without looking up from his plate, August speaks. "I miss April."

"Yeah, me, too," March adds. "When is she coming back home?"

Tucker takes a sip of coffee and puts a forkful of green beans in her mouth. "This 'ere's 'bout th' last of th' green beans we put up last summer. I'll sure miss 'em. Ain't nothin' any better 'n Kentucky Wonder pole beans. Another six weeks 'r so an' we'll be plantin' again."

Silence reclaims the congregation.

After a few moments, August says, "About the only time we get to see April is on the school bus."

March says, "She looks different than she used to. Have you noticed how many times she wears a dress to school?"

"Tucker," August ventures, "I thought you said she was just going to visit Miss Ella for a little while. It's like you've just give her away."

Tucker stops eating. The wind stops blowing. Electricity fills the air.

Slapping the table with the palms of her hands, Tucker makes the dishes rattle. With nostrils flared, she says, "'s'at what y' think? I give 'er away? That just shows how stupid y' both are.

"I'll tell y' what it's like when yore throwed away. M' daddy locked me in th' dog pen fer two weeks when I was a kid, no bigger'n you March. I slept with th' dogs t' stay warm an' ate what they ate t' keep from bein' hungry. April ain't been throwed away!"

15

August and March stare wide-eyed at Tucker.

"Really Tucker?" Augusts asks. "Did your dad really do that to you?"

"Man, that's sorry," March says.

"That's alright," Tucker says. "He got what he deserved in the end."

Turning toward Tucker, August says, "I've never heard you talk about your daddy. What do you mean 'he got what he deserved'?"

"I don't mean nothin'," Tucker replies. "He ain't deservin' of the breath it'd take t' tell it. Now you boys finish yore supper."

August and March drop their heads and pick at their food.

March mumbles something imperceptible.

"Y' got somethin' else t' say?" Tucker challenges him.

Looking at Tucker, March replies, "What's wrong with us? Mama don't want us and now April don't. Is it something we done?"

Tucker looks from one boy to the other. "If'n ya'll ain't th' whiniest coupl'a little girls I ever listened to. Y' need t' grow up and quit feelin' sorry fer yoreself. I ain't raised neither one o' y' t' be some kind o' sissy. Supper's over. Git up 'n clean yore dishes."

Later that night, March and August are lying in their shared bed.

Out of the darkness, March says, "It's because of what we used to do with April. That's why she don't want to have nothing to do with us."

"Shut up," August hisses. "Just shut up."

"You know it's true," March insists.

"I don't know nothing and neither do you," August says. "Besides, we was just playing around. Nobody got hurt."

A silence fills the room that is thicker than the black of the night.

After a few minutes, March says, "I think that's why she never talked."

March feels August move and senses that he is on his elbow, looking in his direction.

August says, "I told you the last time it happened, that we'd never talk about it again." Seizing March around the neck and shaking him, he adds, "Now shut up!"

August flops back on his pillow and jerks the covers over himself.

Both boys lie motionless, lost in their thoughts.

In the stillness, March begins whimpering. After a moment, he bursts out, and in a broken voice, says, "August, you and me is going to burn in hell."

Meanwhile, under the naked light bulb hanging from the ceiling in her bedroom downstairs, Tucker sits on her bed. In her lap are a handful of photographs. One at a time she lays them side by side on her quilt.

The first photograph is a black and white of a smiling, dark-haired, handsome man in overalls. Beside him is a large woman in a plain dress with a scowl on her face. Standing in front of them is a small girl in a dress. The girl is expressionless. Her eyes look dead. In her arms is a small puppy.

The next photograph is a school photograph of a beautiful, dark haired teenage girl. Her shimmering blue eyes have a seductive look about them.

Next is a photograph of a younger August, his kinked hair looking as if each strand has a mind of its own and refuses to be tamed.

Beside it she lays a photograph of a grinning March, with two of his front teeth missing and his dark hair sporting a crooked part down the side.

The last photograph is of April, her blond hair looking unkempt and her lifeless eyes staring back at Tucker.

Tucker picks up the first photograph and holds it beside the one of April. She looks from one girl to the other.

Clutching them to her chest, she begins to sob, "My baby, my baby. I ain't throwed you away. Sleep well this night and know that ol' Tucker loves you."

Chapter Five

Looking out the front window of the house, March calls out, "Tucker, somebody's here!"

From the kitchen, Tucker replies, "Well who is it?"

"It's the social worker, Mary Beth."

Moving as fast as she can, Tucker comes in the living room carrying a large pot and a wooden spoon. She positions herself so she will be hidden when the front door is opened. To March she says, "When she knocks, you open the door and let her in."

Just then, there is a knock at the door. March opens it and says, "Hello Miss Mary Beth. Come on in."

Mary Beth hesitates. "Where is Tucker? I know she's hiding somewhere and is going to try and scare me."

"Tucker said for me to tell you to come in and she'll be here in a minute," March says.

Mary Beth stretches her short leg and sets a foot inside. She looks left and right, then behind her. She calls out, "Tucker! You better not try and scare me!"

Listening carefully, Mary Beth eases into the living room. March walks in front of her and says, "Come on in."

Without looking behind her, Mary Beth closes the door. Just as the door latches, Tucker begins banging the bottom of the pot as hard as she can with her wooden spoon.

Mary Beth screams, throwing her hands into the air. She spins around and attacks Tucker, pounding her thick shoulders.

Feigning hurt, Tucker cries, "Yore killin' me. Pull 'er off March. She'sa killin' me."

August comes running down from upstairs. "What's happening?"

March rolls on the floor, laughing hysterically. He points and says, "Tucker scared Miss Mary Beth again."

August grins broadly.

Hair askew, red-faced, and out of breath, Mary Beth stops hitting Tucker. She straightens her rumpled clothes and says, "One of these days Tucker, I'm going to get you and I mean get you good."

Smiling, Tucker says, "That'll be th' day. How come your 'ere this late'n th' day?"

"I've talked with the folks at school about April and had to come see for myself if it is really true what they are telling me," Mary Beth says. "Is she really talking?"

"Yes she is," March says excitedly.

"It's amazing," August adds. "It's like all the words was stuck in her head and suddenly they started coming out of her mouth."

Tucker returns to the living room from putting her pot and spoon away. "I done always tol' ever'body she wudn't retarded. She's a smart girl."

Smiling, Mary Beth says, "Well where is she? I can't wait to talk with her."

"She ain't here," March begins, "she lives – "

Cutting him off, and giving him a sharp look, Tucker says, "She's visitin' down t' Miss Ella's this a'ternoon. We kin go down there if'n y' wanta."

Mary Beth looks from Tucker to March. "What were you about to say, March?"

"Nothin'."

Grabbing March's arm, August says, "Come on. Let's go get our chores done outside."

As the boys leave, Mary Beth fixes Tucker with a stare. "What's going on Tucker? I know something is going on. You're hiding something, aren't you?"

Ignoring the question, Tucker says, "You wanta see April, or not?"

"You said she is visiting a 'Miss Ella.' Who is she and where does she live?"

"She moved in t' th' McDaniel place last fall. We kin walk down there."

"I'm telling you Tucker, I smell something fishy. And my legs are too short and too old to walk anywhere. Let's drive down there in my car."

Arriving at the McDaniel house and getting out of her car, Mary Beth follows in Tucker's wake to Ella's front door. Mary Beth tries to get past Tucker to the door but Tucker blocks her and knocks on the door.

In a moment, Ella opens the door. Mary Beth darts in front of Tucker, "Hello my name is – "

"This 'ere's Mary Beth the social worker," Tucker completes the introduction, emphasizing the words social worker.

Ella extends her hand. "Hello Mary Beth. My name is Ella. Won't you come in."

Tucker says, "I tol' 'er that April was down 'ere visitin' you this a'ternoon."

Mary Beth rolls her eyes at Tucker.

Speaking to Ella, she says, "Ella, as you may or may not know I made a visit last December to Tucker because of April's lack of progress in school. It's my responsibility to report back to Judge Jack McDade the progress or lack of progress that April has made since I saw Tucker in December. That report is due next week."

Keeping her eyes fixed on Mary Beth, Ella says calmly, "You know I believe I remember Tucker mentioning something about that to me. Let's have a seat here in the living room."

"So where is April?" Mary Beth asks.

"She's in her..........in my spare room," Ella replies. Raising her voice she calls, "April, can you come in here please?"

From within the house a child's voice says, "Yes ma'am."

Mary Beth's eyebrows rise. Looking at Tucker, she mouths, "April?"

Tucker nods solemnly.

April comes skipping into the room, her pigtails bouncing in rhythm. When she sees the audience assembled there, she stops and drops her head.

Ella glances at Tucker who is staring at her.

Taking a deep breath, Ella turns to Mary Beth and says, "Okay. This is silly. My name is Ella McDade, the ex-wife of Judge Jack. And April has been living with me since December."

Tucker blinks rapidly.

Mary Beth fixes Tucker with an expression that says, "Well?" But Tucker is silent.

Turning her attention to April, Mary Beth says, "Do you remember me, April? We've met before."

April nods her head but keeps her attention focused on the floor.

"April," Ella says, "would you like to bring me the autoharp? Maybe Mary Beth would like to hear you sing a song."

April's head snaps up, she flashes a quick smile and says, "I'll be right back." She darts from the room.

Mary Beth opens her briefcase, takes out a note pad and scribbles furiously.

"Whatchu writin'?" Tucker asks.

Not bothering to look up, Mary Beth continues writing. "You don't seem to understand. I've been given the responsibility to see that April receives everything that she needs. I have to fill out reports. I have to go before Judge Jack."

She pauses and looks at them. "How's it going to sound when I tell him that one of the biggest thorns in his side and his ex-wife have teamed up to score a victory? Ever since his accident it seems he's just looking for a reason to throw the book at people. Well, I, for one, don't want to be hit by that book."

"Judge Jack kin go t' hell as fer as I'm concerned," Tucker growls.

"So," Ella counters, "all three of us in this room have the same goal – to help April, right?"

"That's what I want," Tucker says. "What 'bout you Mary Beth?"

"Don't be silly," Mary Beth says. "Of course that's what I want. That's all that matters."

"Well then," Ella continues, "if after your visit here this afternoon you have any doubts that April is being cared for properly, then report those doubts to the court."

Carrying the autoharp case with two hands, April comes into the room, grunting with the effort of holding it up off the floor.

As she hands it to Ella, Ella says, "So what song do you want to do for Mary Beth?"

"I don't care," April says shyly.

"What about that new one we've been working on? Want to try that one?"

April smiles warmly. "Yes."

Ella begins strumming the autoharp rhythmically. "This is an old song, but it's one of my favorites." She nods at April and says, "Whenever you're ready."

Turning to face Tucker and Mary Beth, April opens her mouth and in a voice as brilliant as the North Star on a moonless night, sings, "Hear that lonesome whippoorwill......"

A few minutes later, she sings the last line, "I'm so lonesome I could cry."

The last notes hang in the air like breath on a cold night. The only sound heard is Mary Beth sniffling. She pulls a tattered tissue from her pants, wipes her eyes and blows her nose. She looks at Tucker and sees the streaks of tears on her full cheeks.

Her gaze shifts from Tucker, to Ella, to April. "It's a miracle. That's all I know to say. It's a miracle. Come here April and let me give you a hug."

April walks carefully into Mary Beth's embrace and, looking over Mary Beth's shoulder, smiles at Ella.

~~~~~~~~~~~~~~~~

Chapter Six

Turning in her car seat to look at him, Maisy says, "I had a great time tonight Tiger. I like going up to Fast Eddie's. It's always a fun place to go to. Lots of good food and good music."

"Glad you enjoyed yourself," he says. Glancing toward her, he adds, "You know I've got a name. You always call me 'Tiger.'"

Maisy laughs. "I like calling you Tiger. That's my personal nickname for you. I'm the only one who calls you that, aren't I?"

"You sure are," he replies.

Slipping her hand between his thighs, she says, "And you know why I named you Tiger, don't you?"

Jerking the steering wheel as he jumps, he swerves into the oncoming lane. He quickly pulls back into his lane. "Crazy woman! You could have killed us! You're just lucky it's late at night and there weren't any cars heading our way. Now keep your hands where they belong."

Pulling her thick hair back with both hands, Maisy giggles. "You should have seen your face. Your eyes were as big as half dollars."

He makes no comment, but keeps his hands firmly on the steering wheel.

"Okay," Maisy says, "I promise to behave myself." Smiling, she adds, "At least until we get to the Blue Bank."

They drive in silence for a while, the radio playing music from WLS-AM.

After an hour, he pulls the car into the parking area of the Blue Bank Motel. Going inside the lobby, he pulls his billfold out as he approaches the check-in desk.

The overweight lady behind the desk looks up from reading a

magazine. Winking, she says, "You back again Mr. Smith? Haven't seen you in a few weeks. You want your regular room?"

"Yes," he says. "That'll be fine."

"How long you staying?" she asks.

"One night," he says.

"That'll be thirty-five dollars," she tells him.

Opening his billfold, he takes out a fifty dollar bill and slides it toward her. "Keep the change. And remember – "

"I never saw you," she finishes for him.

Taking the key from her, he says, "Exactly. You're as sweet as those Flippin peaches ya'll are famous for around here. Thanks Rose."

Getting in the car, he drives to the back of the motel. They get out of the car and disappear, hand in hand, into the dark motel room.

An hour later, they are lying side by side in bed.

Maisy says, "Hey Tiger, I think you forgot something last month. I didn't get the usual deposit in my banking account. It must have slipped your mind."

Getting out of the bed, he walks toward a chair. As he walks away from her, he says, "Maisy, we've got to talk."

Maisy's eyes widen and she takes a quick breath, but by the time he sits in the chair facing her, she's quelled the rising panic. With a lilt in her voice, she sits cross-legged on the bed and says, "Talk about what?"

He is quiet, chewing the inside of his cheek. "Okay," he begins, "this is how it is. I'm not going to be able to continue to give you money every month."

The only indication Maisy has heard him is her eyes widening again.

When she doesn't explode, he feels bolder and continues. "You and I have had a great run, Maisy. And I think I've been more than fair with you the past seven years. You know the saying, 'All good things must come – "

He stops speaking as Maisy slowly gets off the bed, never taking her eyes off him. Her fists are clenched. "Who is she? Who are you seeing? I heard talk that you've been out with your secretary Jane Simmons. How old is she? Twenty?"

Wiping his palms on the arm of the chair, he says, "Don't make this harder than it is Maisy. It's not about another woman. It's just time for me to settle down and raise my family. I've got a career to think about."

Maisy laughs. "Don't try to tell me it's because of that cow of a wife you have. Your career, yes, I believe that. But don't try and give me that b.s. about your wife and family. You're way too narcissistic to care about anyone more than yourself."

"Believe what you want," he says. "But I'll never forget our time together. You are the best lay I've ever had."

She closes the distance between them in three quick steps and slaps him. Putting her hands on the arms of his chair, she leans into his face. Hissing, she says, "Now you listen to me. You are not getting rid of me that easy. You owe me! And you're going to continue to pay me. Go ahead and date and screw whoever you want, but you are going to continue making those deposits in my account. Do we understand each other?"

Pushing her aside, he gets out of his chair. "I've told you it's over and I mean it. Now get dressed so I can take you home."

Maisy takes his place in the chair, crosses her legs, and lights a cigarette. Nonchalantly tapping her fingernails on the table, she says, "You ever hear of something called a paternity suit?"

There is an imperceptible moment of motionlessness as he puts a leg in his pants. "I've read about scientists trying to find a test like that, but they've never been admissible in court. They're not reliable."

When Maisy doesn't respond, he slips his shirt on and says, "Why do you ask about that?"

Spinning her lighter on the table, Maisy says, "Oh nothing. I just read something a couple of weeks ago about it. Seems they've recently come up with something that's 90% accurate. I believe it's called HLA typing. Some cases are now being resolved in court using the test."

He stops dressing and faces her. "What kind of game are you plotting? And who is your unsuspecting target?"

"I've got my sights set on the father of my daughter, April," Maisy replies.

Shaking his head, he laughs and says, "That poor sucker. I pity him." He proceeds into the bathroom to comb his hair.

In the reflection of the mirror, he sees Maisy is now leaning against the bathroom door frame.

She says, "Is this some kind of act? Or are you really that stupid?"

Continuing to comb his hair, he replies, "What are you talking – " He stops in mid-sentence and slowly turns to face her. A bead of sweat is on his upper lip.

Grabbing a fistful of his shirt, Maisy says, "Yeah, it's you, you idiot. You are April's father. So you can call it child support, if you want, but the money is not going to stop."

His face flushes and his eyes bulge. He grips her wrist and twists it, loosening her grip on his shirt. He shoves her to the floor. "Listen to me bitch, I could produce a string of men you've slept with that would look like Macy's Thanksgiving Day Parade.

Nobody will believe for one moment that I'm the father. Now get dressed!"

Maisy laughs. Getting up, she says, "You're scared aren't you? Well that's good. You better be because I've already talked to a judge who will be glad to entertain a paternity suit using this new test."

Turning her back to him and picking up her clothes, she adds, "And even if the case gets thrown out by a higher court, it should make sensational headlines in our local newspaper, don't you think? I'll give you a week to make a deposit. If you don't, I'm seeing the judge."

~~~~~~~~~~~~~~~~~

Chapter Seven

A week later, he drives his gray Oldsmobile Cutlass into the driveway of Maisy's apartment. He extinguishes the headlights and shuts off the engine.

Grabbing the steering wheel, he squeezes it until his knuckles turn white. Eventually he jerks his hands free, as if the steering wheel shocked him. Letting out a slow breath, he leans back and puts his head on the headrest.

He pats the breast pocket of his sports jacket and feels the bulge of the plastic bag hidden inside an interior pocket. Making sure there is no passing traffic, he reaches for the door handle and exits the car.

After one knock on Maisy's door, the door slowly opens.

In the dim light he sees Maisy dressed in a tight fitting green sweater, clearly with no bra underneath. It looks as if she was poured into her black jeans. The smell of White Shoulders fills his head.

"Hey Tiger," Maisy says in a sultry voice. "Come on in."

As he steps in, she closes the door behind him.

When he turns to face her, she slowly turns around on her bare feet and says, "How do I look?"

He opens his mouth to reply but only manages a dry cough. Recovering quickly, he says, "Good enough to eat."

Walking to him, Maisy puts her arms around his middle and pulls him close to her. Chuckling she says, "I didn't aim to get you all choked up. Now, give me a kiss."

Putting his hands in her thick, raven hair, he kisses her long and deep.

After a moment, Maisy pushes him back and gasps. "Wow Tiger, a lady has to breath you know! I believe your motor was running before you got here. Slow down a little. Let's have something to drink."

"Sure," he says. "That's a good idea."

As she reaches for the Jack Daniels and glasses, she watches him glancing around her apartment.

"This is your first time here, isn't it? How do you like it?"

"It's nice Maisy," he replies. "It looks like you."

Taking the glasses and bottle with her to the couch, she says, "Come sit down and tell me why you decided you wanted to come to my place after all these years. You get tired of driving back and forth to the Blue Bank?"

Sitting beside her, he drains his drink. "I just thought it would be kind of exciting to meet you on your own ground, instead of sneaking off somewhere."

She pours him another drink and sips hers while she looks at him closely. "By the way," she says, "thanks for making that deposit this week. I thought you'd see things my way after you had time to think it through."

"Let's not talk about all that," he says. "I gave you what you wanted, that's all that matters."

He shifts so that he is facing her. "I thought we might add a little spice to our evening by trying something new."

Maisy's eyes dance. "You know I'm always willing to try new things."

He reaches inside his jacket and pulls out a plastic bag full of capsules.

Frowning, Maisy says, "What's that?"

"They're called Quaaludes," he replies. "My guy says that if you take some before having sex, the result is like nothing you've ever experienced. It's really popular in the big cities and on college campuses."

"I'm not so sure," Maisy says slowly. "Smoking pot with you is one thing, but I don't know about this. I've never heard of it. Have you used it before?"

"No," he says. "That's the whole point of my being here. I wanted my first time doing it to be with you."

An appreciative smile spreads across Maisy's face. "That's my Tiger. Okay, I'm game, if you are."

He opens the bag and takes out two capsules. "Let's each take one and see what happens," he coaches her.

They each slip the capsules in their mouth and wash them down with the whiskey.

"I better go to the little girl's room before we get started," Maisy says.

"Sure, go ahead," he says. "Let's get comfortable."

When she disappears into the bathroom, he takes out the bag of capsules and begins opening them and pouring the powdered contents into Maisy's glass. After the tenth one, he hears the door knob on the bathroom door turn. Sweeping the remaining few capsules into the bag and slipping it back in his jacket, he pours them both a generous portion of Jack Daniels.

Maisy rejoins him on the couch by straddling him and kissing him.

After a few moments, he twists his face from hers. "Whoa girl, remember I've got to breath, too. Let's finish our drinks."

He reaches for the two glasses and hands one to Maisy. "Here's to an unforgettable night."

Maisy clinks her glass against his, empties her glass, and says, "Unforgiveable." Laughing, she says, "I mean, unforgettable. I'm already feeling pretty loose Tiger. Let's head to the bedroom."

He helps her off the couch. She tries to walk but sways clumsily. "Easy," he says as he catches her. "You don't want to fall and hurt yourself."

"I don't feel so good," Maisy says slowly. "Everything is spinning so fast."

"You're going to be fine," he says. "Just relax and enjoy the ride."

Maisy looks at him with unfocused eyes, blinks twice and collapses on the floor.

~~~~~~~~~~~~~~~~

Chapter Eight

Kneeling down, he places two fingers on Maisy's jugular vein. Feeling a faint pulse, he stands up and looks around the room.

Stepping over her, he walks to the coffee table and picks up his glass. Taking out a handkerchief, he wipes the outside of the glass and sets it down, while still holding it with the handkerchief. Picking up the bottle of Jack Daniels, he methodically repeats the process.

He walks to the front door and wipes the inside doorknob, opens the door and wipes the outside doorknob. Closing the door, he walks back to Maisy's body.

Again, he checks her pulse. Feeling nothing, he puts his ear to her chest. When he hears nothing, he smiles.

Pulling her to a sitting position, he puts his shoulder to her midsection, letting her head and arms fall over his shoulder. He grabs her hips and, with a grunt, stands up.

Her weight is more than he calculated and he loses his balance. Sticking out his left hand, he finds a wall and steadies himself.

Walking to the front door, he checks the traffic outside. Seeing no headlights, he uses his handkerchief to grip the doorknob. Opening the door, he steps onto the porch and closes the door behind him.

As he goes down the steps, he loses his balance again but grabs the handrail before falling.

He steps to the rear of his car, finds his keys and opens the trunk, dumping Maisy's body inside. Easing the trunk lid down, he pushes it until it clicks shut.

Panting heavily, he quickly gets inside the driver's seat. His eardrums feel like the bass drum in a marching band and his chest feels as if it will explode any second.

Placing the key in the ignition, he cranks the engine and slowly backs out of the driveway, keeping his headlights off.

He makes his way around the court square and heads north toward Latham. At the last four-way stop before leaving town, a police car pulls in behind him and switches on its solitary, rotating red light.

The flashing red startles him. Looking in the rearview mirror, he sees the officer stepping out of his car. He rolls his window down as the officer approaches.

"Is there a problem officer?" he asks.

The policeman switches on his flashlight. "Oh, it's you sir," the policeman says. "Didn't realize who it was. Are you okay?"

Working to keep his voice calm, he says, "Sure, I'm okay Lloyd. I was just visiting friends and family and heading home. Is there some kind of problem?"

"It's your headlights sir. They aren't burning."

"Wow, thanks Lloyd," he says, while switching them on. "I guess I just forgot. Anything else?"

"That was all," Lloyd says. "I thought I was going to find a drunk driver. You be careful driving home."

"Sure will," he says. "Thanks again."

His hand trembles as he reaches for the gear shift and puts the car in drive. In five minutes the street lights of the city are retreating in his mirror and the darkness of the cloud-filled country sky swallows him.

Twenty minutes later, he drives through the sleeping community of Latham. Once through, he slows, peering intently up ahead.

He crosses a bridge with wooden side rails. He slows and spies another bridge.

Just before crossing it, he brakes and pulls off the road onto a dirt path that leads to the Obion River and its backwater below. Though officially designated a "river," the actual channel of the river is often no more than twenty feet wide.

Empty beer cans are scattered along the path, giving evidence that fishing wasn't the only thing on the minds of those who used the path over the years.

Seeing no other vehicles in the area, he rolls to a stop and turns off the engine. Reaching for the glove compartment, he pulls out a flashlight.

Not as careful now, he gets out of the car and closes the door. Switching on the flashlight, he finds the bank of the river and walks along side it. After about fifty yards, his light discovers what he's been looking for – a Reelfoot boat fitted with an engine.

He sweeps his light across the length the boat bottom and sees the concrete blocks and rope he'd placed there earlier.

He'd chosen a Reelfoot boat because of its ability to get past stumps and limbs that hover just beneath the surface of the water. Untying it from the tree, he pushes it into the water and gets inside. He finds the lawnmower engine sitting a third of the way from the rear of the boat, with its long shaft protruding over the back of the boat. The engine starts with the second pull of the rope.

Using his flashlight, he steers a course back to the bridge, pulls up on the bank and shuts off the engine. Making his way to the trunk of his car, he opens it. The dim trunk light falls on Maisy's ashen face. He thinks he sees her smirk and checks her pulse again before pulling her out.

Shaking his head because his imagination got the best of him, he lifts her on his shoulder and walks to the boat. Leaning forward, he lets her body fall into the boat.

Grunting, he pushes the heavy load into the stream and gets inside. Cranking the engine, he makes his way along the meandering path of the timber-lined Obion. Occasionally he switches on his flashlight to get his bearings, but mostly he travels in the dark.

The only sounds are of the engine and the bottom of the boat hitting downed limbs or submerged stumps.

After thirty minutes, he turns the boat out of the main stream into a flooded open area thick with lily pads. As the boat slides through the lily pads, he cuts the engine off.

Squatting and keeping hold of both sides of the boat with both hands, he eases toward the middle of the boat where Maisy lies. He sits on his knees, picks up a concrete block and a piece of rope. One end of the rope he ties to her ankle and the other to the block.

He continues until he's tied a block to each of her ankles, knees, and wrists. Wiping his perspiring face, he takes a longer piece of rope and ties it around her waist and attaches two concrete blocks to the other end. The final block he ties around her neck.

Looking at his handiwork, he says, "We said it was going to be an unforgettable night, didn't we Maisy? Well we were right."

He drops the blocks tied to her ankles over the side. Her body slides until her knees catch on the side. Lifting the next pair of blocks, he lets them splash into the water. The heavy blocks disappear and jerk Maisy's body after them. She would have disappeared then, but the blocks tied around her waist stop her progress.

Bending her like a pretzel, he takes the two blocks tied to her wrists and swings them over the side, quickly grabbing the one around her neck and casting it after them. The combined weight of Maisy's dead body and of the concrete blocks jerks the side of the boat down so far that he loses his balances and is thrown head first into the inky water.

Maisy's body falls out on top of him, dragging him to the bottom and pinning him face down in the mud ten feet below. Kicking and screaming, he frees himself from his own death trap and swims to the top of the water.

As the fresh air hits his face, he gasps, drawing in both air and water. Choking on the water, while trying to find enough air to stay alive, he treads water, trying to see above the giant lily pads and find his boat.

Frantic, something bumps the back of his head. He yells in fright. Turning around, it is his boat. Grabbing the side rail, he hangs on until he catches his breath.

Swimming to the rear of the boat, he pulls himself in and collapses in the bottom. As his body begins shivering, it dawns on him that, even though the air temperature is warm for February, hypothermia is a threat. He quickly starts the boat and finds his way back to the bridge and his car.

As he gets out of his boat, the clouds break and the full moon forces the blackness of night to hide under the bridge. Opening the door to his car, he pauses and looks at the moon. His face is lit in its soft glow.

Sitting silently under the bridge on the other side of the river, a fishing pole in one hand and a bottle of bourbon in a paper bag in the other, is Smiley Carter.

~~~~~~~~~~~~~~~~~~~~

Chapter Nine

Standing in front of her mirror, April pulls the brush through her shiny, blond hair. She sees her bed behind her, with its Strawberry Shortcake Dolls arranged neatly on the pillow. Still looking in the mirror, she moves until she sees the poster of Big Bird.

Laying the brush down, she walks to her closet and opens the door. She lets her fingertips graze each garment as she moves her hand from left to right. Kneeling down, she matches and lines up all six pairs of her shoes.

She hears Ella taking her nightly shower, a habit April has resisted imitating.

Walking into the kitchen, she looks out the window over the sink toward Tucker's house. A faint light can be seen shining through Tucker's bedroom window. April can suddenly smell the familiar smoky interior mixed with the pungent body odor of Tucker and her brothers.

Having the sensation that they are in the room with her, she spins around. Standing in her bathrobe, with a towel around her head, is Ella.

"Thinking about Tucker and your brothers?" Ella asks.

"Kind of," April replies.

Ella takes her hand. "Let's go sit on the couch."

Sitting down, Ella takes April into her arms and pulls her onto her lap, facing her. "Do you miss them?" she asks.

April nods slowly and then shakes her head.

"Now that's not the way we do it, is it? We're supposed to use our words, right? Get them out of our head?" Ella prompts her. "What are you wanting to say?"

"Sometimes I miss them," April says. "And sometimes I

don't. I ain't never – "

"You haven't ever," Ella corrects her.

"I haven't ever," April begins again, "had such nice clothes and things. And I for sure haven't ever been so clean."

Ella laughs. "I guess you must think I'm awfully silly sometimes. I just can't get out of my head the saying my mother had, which was, 'Cleanliness is next to godliness.'"

"What is godliness?" April asks.

"Well let's see," Ella says. "How best to explain it........I guess it means you try to live godly or to be like God."

Her blues eyes intent on Ella, April asks, "What is God?"

"You mean, who is God?" Ella replies. "Not what, but who."

"Who is God?" April asks.

Smiling, Ella says, "You certainly have your grandmother's trait of asking whatever is on your mind, don't you? I believe God created our world. He made the earth, sun, moon and stars. And he made the first man and woman."

"Where is he?" April asks.

"He lives in a place called heaven," Ella replies.

"Where is heaven?" April asks.

"It's in a place that we can't see. I'm not sure exactly where," Ella tells her.

April searches Ella's face.

Smiling, Ella folds April to her chest. "I love your little inquisitive mind. Asking questions is a good thing. It's how you learn. Now tell me what had you thinking about Tucker and your brothers."

Keeping her cheek resting against Ella, April asks, "Are you my family now?"

Ella's voice catches in her throat. She begins to cry.

April sits up quickly and looks at Ella with concern. "What's wrong? Did I do something wrong?"

Wiping her tears, Ella says, "No, no April. You rarely do anything wrong. In fact, most of the time you do everything just right. I just get emotional sometimes.

"You know," Ella continues, "I've told you I have a son named Cade. But I hardly ever see him. And of course I'm divorced. So it's sort of like I've lost my family. Having you live with me has made me very happy."

April lays her head back on Ella's chest. Speaking softly, she says, "And I have a mama, but she doesn't want me. She gave me to Tucker."

"It's been complicated for you, I know," Ella says. "But Tucker and your brother's love you and they are your family. But maybe you and I can be a family, too."

April sits up. "I can have two families?" she asks.

"You can, if you want to," Ella tells her. "And you can love both families and you can miss them when you are away from them. Now, why don't we have us a glass of warm milk?"

Ella starts to get up but stops. "You'll have to walk. You're too big a girl for me to carry."

She finds a pot in the kitchen and places it on the stove. Getting the milk from the refrigerator, she pours some into the pot and turns on the eye.

April gets two glasses out of the cabinet and places them on the counter.

The creaking and pinging of the warming pot is the only sound in the kitchen as April and Ella are lost in their thoughts.

Finally, Ella lifts the pot and pours some milk into each glass. She and April sit across from each other at the table.

Ella says, "I'll tell you what. You haven't been to Tucker's in a couple of weeks. Tomorrow is Saturday. Why don't we go to Tucker's and let you spend the day there, if you want to? Would you like that?"

Smiling, April says, "Yeah. I want to."

"Okay then," Ella says lightly. "Let's finish our milk and then off to bed."

April lifts her glass and empties it, leaving a white moustache on her lip. Ella laughs and says, "Okay, little kitten, you need to lick your lip."

April's pink tongue darts out and removes the white trimming.

Ella takes their glasses and puts them in the sink. April takes Ella's hand and leads her into her bedroom. When Ella pulls back the Strawberry Shortcake comforter, April hops quickly into the bed.

Bending down, Ella kisses April on the forehead. "Sleep tight beautiful girl. Always remember, you are special."

Smiling, April closes her eyes.

Ella walks into her own bedroom and pulls back her covers. She sits on the side of the bed, slips off her house shoes, and gets in.

Lying on her back, she lets out a long sigh. "Dear Lord, Where is this incredible journey you have me on going to take me? You gave me the strength to escape my horrible marriage. You delivered me from cancer. Then you plop me into the middle of Tucker's life. And now you've given me the blessing of April. Help me to not be selfish in my attitude and feelings toward this little angel. Give me wisdom to know what to do and say with her.

And protect us all. In Jesus name, Amen."

Rolling on her side, she closes her eyes and falls asleep.

~~~~~~~~~~~~~~~~

Chapter Ten

Walking to Tucker's the next morning, Ella says to April, "Look at that beautiful blooming dogwood at the edge of the woods."

"Which one is the dogwood?" April asks.

"The one with the white blooms," Ella replies. "And that purple one next to it is a redbud tree. I love how beautiful spring is out here in the country, don't you?"

Spying a clump of blooming daffodils in the ditch beside the road, April jumps in and picks a handful. Climbing back out of the ditch, she stretches her handful of flowers toward Ella and says, "These are for you."

Smiling, Ella says, "Thank you. Why don't we take these to Tucker?"

"Tucker doesn't care about flowers," April responds. "She'll think it's silly to put flowers on a table like you do."

Keeping her voice light, Ella says, "That's okay. I'll carry them and be sure we take them back home after our visit. I think they're lovely, just like you."

April smiles and takes Ella's hand.

As they approach Tucker's house, they hear an engine in the direction of the barn. Looking in that direction, Ella sees Smiley Carter and his tractor in the garden. Tucker is standing on one end of the garden. March and August are coming out of the barn.

"I wonder what's going on?" she asks aloud.

April pulls on her hand and says excitedly, "Let's go see."

When they are fifty yards from the barn April calls out, "Tucker!" Smiley Carter's tractor drowns out April's tiny voice. Letting go of Ella's hand, she breaks into a run.

She darts past August and March as they carry hoes and rakes from the barn to the garden. They both holler at her sprinting figure, "April!"

Catching a movement out of the corner of her eye, Tucker turns. April is twenty feet away, running full speed toward her with open arms. Simultaneously they call each other's name. Bending down, Tucker catches April as she leaps into her strong arms.

Tucker stumbles a bit under the unexpected force of April's enthusiastic greeting. Her thick arms encircle April's small frame.

April buries her face in Tucker's neck and inhales through her nose, taking in the mixture of familiar odors – fried meat from breakfast, hogs from feeding, body odor from sweating, and the earthy smell of the garden. She whispers, "I missed you."

Pulling April's arms from around her neck and setting her down, Tucker says, "Y' come on a good day. We's plantin' crowder peas t'day. May's th' month fer plantin' peas, y' know."

Smiley Carter and his tractor reach them at the same time March and August arrive. Carter shuts off the engine and exclaims, "Well lookee here what done come to see ol' Smiley Carter. It's the princess April."

August and March stand a couple of feet away. "Hey April," August says.

"Whata you been doin'?" March asks.

Looking at the boys, Tucker says, "What's amatter with you two? Git on up 'ere an' see yore sister. Y' ack like strangers."

April positions her back against Tucker's thigh and faces her brothers.

Ignoring everyone, Carter strides toward April and says, "Well I's ain't no stranger to the princess." As April smiles at him, he picks her up and pitches her into the air, extracting a squeal of delight from her. He catches her and cradles her like a baby. "You's still the prettiest chil' I done ever see'd."

Ella edges quietly into the gathering.

August notices her first. "Hey Miss Ella," he says.

Everyone turns.

"Hi August. Hi everyone," Ella says. "My grandfather used to throw me into the air just like that, Smiley Carter. I still remember feeling like my stomach was going to jump out of my mouth."

Tucker says, "Yeah, but Carter here's a broken down ol' man an' he's gonna drop her one o' these times."

Carter pushes his sleeves up, flexes his biceps and says, "Does that look like a broken down ol' man? I can still work circles round men half my age."

"An' it's time w' all git busy n' plant these peas," Tucker says. Looking at Carter she says, "Y' think y' got that ground worked up good enough?"

Waving his hand toward the area he has disked up, Carter says, "That garden is cut up as fine as coffee grounds. You's can probably just throw that seed at the ground and it'll sink in all's by itself."

"If'n hot air makes fer good ground," Tucker replies, "then it'll be th' best around after listenin' t' you.

"August, you n' March git the hoes n' start layin' off them rows. Me n' Ella'll plant th' seed."

August and March respond quickly and begin sliding their hoes through the soft soil, leaving a furrow in the wake. Tucker picks up a paper sack, reaches inside and brings out a handful of small seeds. Ella watches closely and imitates Tucker's moves.

Watching August and March, Tucker calls to them, "You boys

make 'em rows straight." Pointing to one row, she adds, "This 'n here's as crooked as a dog's hind leg."

She begins carefully dropping the seeds into the furrow. "You take that row beside mine, Ella."

Ella dutifully obeys and begins dropping seeds in.

Carter says, "I'll just grab me a rake and cover up them seeds." With a wink at Ella he adds, "But not too deep. Don't wanta smother 'em."

Catching his meaning, Tucker says, "You jest look over at 'em taters 'n tell me which plants look the best, them y' planted shaller er them what I planted right."

Shaking his head, Carter laughs and says to Ella, "See whats I's gots to puts up with? This woman always thinks she's right. There ain't no point in tryin' to reason with her."

For the next few minutes, everyone works in silence.

Finally, Tucker says, "What brung you an' April over here, Ella?"

Keeping her focus on planting, Ella replies, "I think she was a little homesick last night. So I promised her we'd come visit today."

When Tucker gives no response, Ella continues, "I can't remember the last time she saw her mother."

Tucker spits and says, "She's better off not seein' 'er. B'sides, I can't 'member th' last time I seen Maisy. She didn't come see March 'r April fer their birthdays. As selfish as she is, that wuz at least one thing she always done."

She stops and cocks her head to one side, looking at the sky. "I guess I ain't seen 'er since th' end o' January. Hmmmm. That is a long time, even fer Maisy."

Ella stops, too, and looks at Tucker. "Do you think she is

okay?"

"How am I supposed t' know?" Tucker snaps. "She ain't never seen fit t' tell me nothin' 'bout what's goin' on with her."

Tucker looks at Carter who is leaning on his rake and looking at her. "Whut'r you lookin' at?"

"I's just waitin' for you two to get movin' again," Carter says. "I can't cover up a row that ain't got no seed in it."

Both women turn and start sowing the seed into the welcoming furrows.

After a few minutes, Ella says, "If you want to Tucker, I can drive you to where Maisy lives, just to be sure everything is alright."

"I ain't never knowed where she lives," Tucker replies. "She ain't never tol' me. All I got is a phone number she give me one time. I don' know why. I ain't never had no use fer phones."

"Well," Ella says, "there is a way I can use her phone number and get an address for where she lives, if you want me to."

"You can if y' wanta," Tucker replies. "But I'll bet she's finally run off with some man. Ain't no tellin' where to."

<center>~~~~~~~~~~~~~~~</center>

Chapter Eleven

Sitting on her couch the following Monday morning, Ella picks up the receiver on her phone and dials 411. After a moment she says, "Could I speak to Rebecca Wallace, please?

"Hello Becky? This is Ella McDade.......Fine thanks. And you?........That's great. Listen, I need to ask a favor of you. I have a phone number here that I want to find the address to."

She unfolds the paper Tucker gave her on Saturday and reads the numbers to Rebecca. There is a long pause.

"Really? And that was the last you heard from them?..........Give me that address one more time........Thanks a bunch Becky." She hangs up the phone.

Staring at the address, she purses her lips and frowns. She stands up and slips the paper into her pocket. Walking to the front door, she takes her car keys off the hook and heads outside.

Within a few moments she drives into Tucker's front yard. Getting out of her car, she notices Tucker coming from behind the house.

As Ella gets out of her car, Tucker says, "What's got you out early on a Monday mornin'?"

"I checked out that phone number Maisy gave you," Ella replies.

"What'dja learn?" Tucker asks.

"Well the first thing they told me was that the phone number had been disconnected because the bill wasn't paid. The last payment they received was in March."

"Hmph," Tucker grunts. "Don't surprise m' none. Her sugar daddy o' th' month must 'o missed a payment."

"Maybe," Ella says, "but I've got an address we can go check out and see for ourselves what's going on."

"I ain't got nothin' else t' do," Tucker agrees.

Ten minutes later, Ella turns on to Maple Street. "It's somewhere down this street. I'm just not sure which end of the street it is."

Scanning the house numbers, Ella says, "We're looking for 417."

Tucker keeps her focus on the street.

"There it is!" Ella says excitedly. She pulls slowly into the driveway. Dozens of unopened newspapers, in varying shades of decaying yellow, lie scattered in the front yard and on the driveway.

As they get out of the car, Tucker says, "What's all them rolls of things in th' yard?"

"Looks like she was getting the daily newspaper," Ella answers. "But she hasn't picked them up in weeks. Sometimes people pay for their paper three months at a time, so I guess they've just on kept delivering them."

The two women slowly approach the steps to the front door.

"Isn't that her car?" Ella asks, pointing.

"It's th' last 'n I seen 'er in," Tucker replies.

They arrive at the front door and look at each other. "Why don't you knock?" Ella suggests.

Tucker strikes the door twice with the bottom of her fist.

When nothing happens, Tucker grabs the door knob and tries to turn it, but it doesn't yield.

Ella says, "Something doesn't feel right." Peering through the rectangular window of the door, she says, "I don't see any lights. Let's walk around the house and see if we can see anything through the windows."

"I'm tellin' y' she done run off," Tucker says. "Jus' like m' mama done."

Looking at Tucker, Ella says, "What do you mean?"

Tucker waves her hand and says, "Nothin.' Never mind." Lumbering down the steps, she says, "We'll walk aroun' th' house an' check, like you said."

After making their way from window to window, Ella says, "Everything is still there - furniture, clothes, appliances. She wouldn't have left those behind, if she was moving away. And the electric meter was pulled. I'll bet we'll hear the same story on that as we heard about the phone."

"So what'r we gonna do now?" Tucker asks.

"Let's go see Ron Harris," Ella says. "He'll know what to do."

"Y' mean th' sheriff?" Tucker asks.

Walking toward her car, Ella says, "Sure. Come on."

When Tucker doesn't follow her, Ella turns around to face Tucker. "What's the matter?" she asks.

"Me 'n th' sheriff ain't always seen eye t' eye," Tucker says. "It might not be sech a good idee fer me t' go there."

"Oh come on," Ella urges her. "I've known Ron for years. It'll be fine."

A few minutes later, they pull up to the front of the sheriff's office. A deputy is coming out of the door when he spies Tucker getting out of the car. His eyes widen and he quickly ducks back into the office.

When Ella and Tucker stride into the office, Ella is startled to see four armed deputies lined up side by side along one wall. There is a hard look on each of the deputies' faces. The tension in the air is thick.

Tucker folds her arms across her chest and returns their stares.

Ella sees Tucker's stance and steps between her and the deputies. "Hi Frank. Hi Eddie. How have you been Kerry? How's your family Roy?"

Each deputy gives a polite nod in Ella's direction but they keep their eyes on Tucker.

Ignoring everyone's posturing, Ella continues, "Is Ron in? We need to see him about something."

One of the deputies replies, "I told him who was coming."

At that moment a dark complexioned, bald-headed man with black rimmed glasses, wearing a white shirt, black tie and black pants walks into the room. Stepping in front of the deputies, he extends his hand toward Ella and says, "Hello Ella. It's been a while."

Shaking his hand, Ella smiles and replies, "Yes it has Ron. How have you been?"

"Oh, just staying busy," the sheriff replies. "You know how it is."

He looks past Ella at Tucker, then back at Ella and says, "Are you two here together?"

"Yes we are Ron," Ella says, "and we'd like a few moments of your time, if you can spare it."

"Okay," he replies. "Ya'll come on back to my office."

As he turns and walks away, Ella and Tucker follow him. The four deputies follow them in two's.

Tucker smiles.

Glancing back at the sound of all the shoes, Ella says, "Oh really Ron. Is that necessary?"

Opening his office door for Ella, Ron says, "I think it's okay boys. Ya'll go on about your business."

As the door closes behind him, Ron says, "Ya'll have a seat." He moves behind his desk and sits in his chair accompanied by its complaining squeaks.

"Now, what's on your all's minds?"

Ella explains to him Maisy's recent lack of contact with her children and their learning of her phone and electricity being cut off. "We went to her apartment and found it locked with her car parked in the driveway. Then we looked in the windows and saw that everything is in place as if she evaporated."

She waits for a response from Ron.

Thinking there must be something more, he says, "And your point is?"

"Honestly Ron," Ella says, exasperated. "You need to investigate to see if she's alright."

Ron looks for a long moment at Tucker, then looks at Ella and says, "Listen, you may not know Maisy's history. She's not the most dependable or predictable person. I mean, I could give you a list of men you could call to see if she's with one of them.

"Now Tucker," he quickly adds, "I don't mean no harm. But you know I'm telling the truth."

Looking at Ella, Tucker stands and says, "I toldja. This 's been a waste o' time."

Ella looks at Ron incredulously. "You mean you aren't going to do a thing?"

Turning his palms upward, Ron says, "What do you want me to do?"

Ella's face reddens. "If I've got to tell you how to do your job, then maybe it's time we get us a new sheriff."

She joins Tucker standing and says, "Let's go."

Before she closes the door behind her she turns and says, "I'm telling you right now, Ron Harris, that I've got a bad feeling about this. I think something's wrong."

He stands up and says, "Oh come on now Ella, don't – "

The slamming door cuts of the rest of his reply.

~~~~~~~~~~~~~~~~~~~~

Chapter Twelve

Leaning his head out the driver's window, sixteen year old Gary Winslow watches the rear tires of his pickup truck as he backs toward the bank of the Obion River. The twelve foot aluminum jon boat clangs in the bed of his truck.

Gary's companion, and best friend, sixteen year old Ricky Fields, cracks his passenger door and watches as well.

Slowing, Gary says, "That looks good to me. What about your side?"

Getting out of the truck, Ricky takes a few steps away from the truck and surveys the situation. "Yeah, looks good to me, too."

Braking to a stop, Gary puts on the emergency brake and cuts the engine.

They untie the ropes that have held the boat in place, and, each grabbing a side, slide the boat backwards until the rear drops to the ground. Then they push it into the edge of the water, leaving the bow on shore.

"Doesn't look like anyone else has been in here today," Gary says.

"We'll have it all to ourselves," Ricky says. "This is going to be a blast!"

"Whooo weeee!" Gary exclaims. "I can't wait."

They walk quickly back to the truck. Opening their doors, they lower the back of the front seat and take out their bows and arrows.

"Lock your door," Gary says.

Ricky pushes down the lock and closes his door, checking the door button to be sure it is secure. He reaches inside the bed of the truck and lifts out a small cooler.

Gary grabs a cooler as well. "You get in the boat first and I'll push us in," he says.

Getting in, Ricky steps to the back of the boat. Each boy lays his bow and cooler in the middle of the boat.

Grabbing a paddle, Ricky says, "Push us off matey!"

Gary grips the front of the boat and bends low, pushing with his legs. He gains speed with each step. Suddenly the boat is freed from being moored to the ground and slides easily into the water. Leaping into the boat, Gary grabs the other paddle.

As they begin paddling, Ricky shouts, "Alligator gar, here we come! Be prepared to surrender to the bow fishing champions of the world!"

Gary bursts out laughing.

In a few moments they leave the brilliant June sun in the opening by the bridge and ease into the cool shade of the tree-lined channel. Both boys take in the quiet stillness.

"Don't forget," Gary says, "my dad says to be one the lookout for snakes hanging on branches. They love to drop in the boat."

Brandishing a large hunting knife, Ricky says, "Just let 'em come. I'll cut their heads off!"

Laughing, Gary says, "Sure you will. More than likely you'll jump out of the boat and let me fend for myself."

They row for a ways in silence.

Suddenly Ricky says, "Up there on the left. That's what we're looking for."

Gary looks to where Ricky is pointing. A large area, thick with lily pads, lies in the open sunlight.

"My granddaddy," Ricky continues, "says those beds of lily pads are where gar like to stay. He said it may look like there's no water there, but it's probably six to eight feet deep this time of year."

The boys paddle their way out of the shade. They grab their sunglasses as the dazzling sun blinds them.

Slipping off their white t-shirts, they reveal tan lines at their sleeves and collar. They grasp their bows. Each checks the reel on the front of the bow to be sure the fishing line will release freely. Then they tie the end of the line to an arrow.

"You want me to skull first, or you," Gary asks.

"I'll go first," Ricky says

Gary carefully stands up. Smiling, he says, "Let the games begin."

Keeping his paddle under water at the back of the boat, Ricky works it slowly back and forth. The boat silently glides into the bed of lily pads.

After a few minutes, Gary whispers, "Easy. I see one."

Ricky keeps his paddle still.

Gary tenses. He slips the arrow onto the bowstring and slowly pulls it back to his cheek. The stretching bowstring emits a low hum in response to the tension.

Without warning, Gary's fingers release the bowstring and the arrow flies invisibly, disappearing into the water with barely a splash, the fishing line spinning off the reel. He quickly grips the handle on the reel.

"Did you get him?" Ricky asks.

Keeping his eyes glued to the spot his arrow disappeared, Gary replies, "I can't tell."

For a moment nothing happens.

Abruptly the line tightens and the bow is nearly jerked out of Gary's hand. "Oh I got him alright!" he yells.

The taught fishing line moves from left to right, the lily pads dancing out of the way of the thrashing fish below.

As if he were being controlled by a marionette, Gary's arms are jerked first one way and then another.

"Hold him!" Ricky yells as Gary almost loses his grip on his bow.

Gary begins reeling in the fish with his right hand, while his left firmly grasps his bow.

Suddenly the feathered end of Gary's arrow makes a dancing appearance among the lily pads.

Reaching toward the arrow shaft, Ricky says, "He's tiring. Just take it easy now."

Gary guides his prey toward the edge of the boat. Ricky grabs the arrow and lifts the fish out of the water. The sun reflects off its thick, redish-orange scales as he drops it in the bottom of the boat.

Sitting down, Gary says, "Oh my gosh, I'll bet it weighs ten pounds!"

"It looks like it's three feet long!" Ricky says. Grabbing his bow, he adds, "Now it's my turn."

Two hours later, the bottom of their boat is littered with gar. Their backs and shoulders are burned a bright red. Sitting in opposite ends of the boat, they both drink their cokes and eat the remains of the sandwiches they brought.

"Man I'm worn out," Ricky says. "We better start heading back to the truck."

"I know," Gary agrees. "But I want to take one last shot."

Grinning, Ricky says, "Okay. But just one."

Slowly Gary rises and begins looking in the lily pads. After a few minutes of Ricky skulling him through the water, he whispers, "Oh yeah, there's what I've been looking for. It looks like the granddaddy of them all lying there."

Ricky lets the boat drift on its own as Gary draws his bow.

Gary flinches and loses his grip. The arrow darts into the water. Slapping his neck, he says, "Stupid sweat bee! Just as I was getting set, the thing stung me. I know I missed the fish."

Laying his bow down, he grabs the fishing line and brings it in by hand. When the arrow appears, he seizes the shaft and begins lifting it.

"Something is on here," he says, "but it's not a fish."

As the end of the arrow comes out of the water, there is a wad of dark green on the arrow head.

"Looks like a wad of moss to me," Ricky says.

Gary grabs the green to remove it and says, "I don't know what this is, but it isn't moss. And it feels like there's a rope or something here, too."

He hands it to Ricky who pulls it toward him. A rope appears from the lily pads, its end disappearing in the murky water.

"What the heck?" Gary says.

Pulling with both hands, Ricky says, "Whatever it is, it's heavy. Help me pull."

Both boys clutch the slimy rope and begin pulling. In response to their efforts, the boat begins moving toward the point where the rope disappears in the lily pads.

"Maybe somebody hid a money chest down here, or something," Gary says.

Laughing, Ricky says, "If it is, it's a fifty-fifty split."

They reach the point where the rope's descent is directly below them. Heaving with all their might, they begin lifting it toward the surface.

While peering over the edge of the boat as they pull, the lily pads abruptly part and the boys stare into the empty sockets of the bloated, smirking face of Maisy.

~~~~~~~~~~~~~~~~~~

Chapter Thirteen

Leaning on her hoe, Tucker pulls a handkerchief from her hip pocket and swipes her sweating face. Stuffing the handkerchief into its home, she surveys her morning's work.

The weeds and grass that had recently stood among her peas now lie limp between the rows, having surrendered to her sharp hoe. In the hot sun their deep green is already fading and the roots are turning brown.

Small clouds of dust surround Tucker's feet as she walks through her garden to the side of the barn. Squatting in the shade, she picks up a quart jar, unscrews the lid and drinks deeply. Some of the refreshing water slips from the corners of her overanxious mouth and runs down her thick neck.

Pausing to catch her breath, Tucker leans her head forward and pours the rest of the water on the back of her neck.

Standing up, she notices a sheriff's patrol car leaving Ella's house and heading toward her own. It pulls into her front yard. August and March come out on the front porch to meet the driver as he approaches the house.

Tucker watches as they point in her direction and sees the driver shield his eyes as he looks toward her.

Getting back in his car, the driver turns around and heads toward Tucker's barn. He coasts the last few yards, stops and shuts off his engine. The door opens and Sheriff Ron Harris steps out. His sweat-soaked white shirt sticks to his chest and back.

Donning a tan Stetson hat, he calls out, "Tucker, you around here?"

Stepping out the shade of the barn, Tucker says, "I am."

Sheriff Harris turns and spots her at the end of her garden. Walking slowly toward her, he says, "There you are. The boys said you was down here somewhere."

Tucker retreats from the heat of the sun by stepping back into the shade.

When he gets a few feet from her, the Sheriff stops. He uses his shirt sleeve to wipe the sweat off his upper lip. "It's gonna be a hot one today, isn't it?"

Tucker notices dried mud on the side of his face. "I spec' so," she replies.

Looking at her garden, he says, "My goodness, that's one of the best gardens I've seen anywhere around. What's your secret?"

"Hogs," Tucker replies.

"Huh?" he says.

"Hogs. Y' asked m' what m' secret was an' I said, 'Hogs.' Can't y' keep up with th' conversation?"

Even though it is shadowed by his Stetson hat, Tucker sees the sheriff's dark face redden.

Taking off his hat, the sheriff says, "I came to see you for a reason."

"Figgered as much," Tucker replies. "Why don'chu git on withit?"

Shifting his weight, he says, "It's about Maisy."

"Figgered that, too," Tucker says.

"Two boys was out bow fishing for carp today and they found a body." He pauses, waiting for a reaction. When Tucker's stony face remains fixed, he adds, "Turns out it was Maisy."

"'ppears Miss Ella was right, don't it?" Tucker says. "Maybe if'n you'd took 'er serious, Maisy might be alive now."

She gives time for the weight of her accusation to settle on the sheriff's shoulders. Then she says, "Where'd y' find 'er?"

"You know that branch of the Obion north of Latham? She was about two miles from the bridge in a field of lily pads."

Tucker's head snaps toward the sheriff. "North o' Latham?" she asks.

Noticing the change in her demeanor, he says, "Yeah. Does that area mean something to you?"

Just as quickly as her interest peaked at his story, Tucker takes a dispassionate stance again. "Nope. Don't mean nothin' t' me? How'd she die?"

"Well," the sheriff begins, "the exact cause of death will have to be determined by the state coroner's office in Memphis. But there's no doubt she was murdered."

"What makes y' say that?" Tucker asks.

Slipping his hat back on, the sheriff shifts his weight. "I'm not sure you need to know those details."

With an edge in her voice, Tucker says, "I got a right t' know what happened t' my daughter."

Taking a deep breath, the sheriff says, "Somebody tied concrete blocks to her and threw her into that backwater. But she could have already been dead. That's what the coroner will have to decide."

In a far away voice, Tucker says, "Concrete blocks...."

The sheriff cocks his head to one side, waiting for Tucker to say more. When she falls silent, he asks, "Do you know anyone who would have wanted to hurt Maisy?"

Tucker scoffs. "I 'magine you know more 'bout th' goin's on of Maisy than me. She didn't never talk t' me 'bout 'er life."

"Well, when was the last time you saw Maisy?"

"I reckon it was sometime in Feb'rary," Tucker replies. "She didn' come see March 'r April fer their birthdays. That's sorta what got Ella thinkin' there might be somthin' wrong. You do remember us comin' t' see you, don'chu?"

"Look Tucker," he says. "Ya'll were right. There was something wrong. But my guess is she was already dead by the time you came asking for help."

Fixing him with a stare, Tucker spits a stream of tobacco juice that just misses his mud-caked boots. She notices him clinching his hands into fists. She grips her hoe tightly.

The sheriff eases his right hand to the butt of his holstered pistol. "Now look Tucker," he says, "let's not make things worse than they already are."

"All o' you, an' ever'one like you, ain't nuthin'but a bunch of sorry – "

"Tucker." Ella's voice inserts a comma into the tension of the scene.

So focused had they been on each other that neither the sheriff nor Tucker had seen Ella walking toward them.

Stepping between them, Ella faces Tucker and says, "The sheriff stopped by my house on the way up here and told me what happened. I'm so very, very sorry."

Taking advantage of Ella's interference, the sheriff takes a couple of steps back. "Listen, there's going to be a full investigation. We'll have to seal Maisy's house. So you won't be able to go over there without a deputy, at least not until we've finished. Until then, if you think of anything that might be helpful, give my office a call."

Both women ignore him.

"And one more thing," he continues, "I'm afraid you'll have to go to the emergency room of the hospital to identify the body."

Tucker looks past Ella at the sheriff and says through gritted teeth, "To hell with you."

Placing her hand on Tucker's arm, Ella says, "We'll be in in a little while Ron. Why don't you go on now."

~~~~~~~~~~~~~~~~

Chapter Fourteen

Peering intently into Tucker's scratch-covered glasses, Ella says, "I'm so sorry Tucker. And I regret that my hunch something was wrong turned out to be right. It's just awful news."

Though Tucker's expression remains unchanged, Ella feels her arm begin to tremble. Suddenly Tucker grasps Ella's forearm. Ella resists the urge to wince in pain at Tucker's iron grip.

Tucker gasps and holds her breath. She finally exhales, then gasps two quick breaths. Her body shudders.

Stepping closer to Tucker, Ella says, "Can I hug you?"

Tucker relinquishes her grip on Ella and drops her hands to her side.

Lifting her arms slowly, Ella places them around Tucker's neck and says, "Poor Tucker."

Tucker unties a chain from her heart and lays her head on Ella's shoulder. Her breathing becomes ragged. A moan emits from deep within her.

Patting Tucker's back, Ella says, "Yes, let it go. Go ahead and cry."

Tucker raises her stiff arms and puts them around Ella's waist. Her moan grows into words, "Maisy, Maisy, Maisy....." Tears begin streaming down her tanned cheeks, leaving tracks in the dust left there from her work in the garden.

Feeling the damp warmth of Tucker's tears on her shoulder, Ella slowly sways left and right. She touches Tucker's coarse, greasy hair. "Sometimes crying is the best thing for the soul."

All of a sudden, Tucker steps back from Ella. Grabbing her chest, she stumbles backward a few more steps.

"Tucker?" Ella says.

Bending at the waist, Tucker continues gripping her chest. Like a wounded animal, her knees buckle and she tumbles to the ground.

"Tucker!" Ella screams.

Hurrying to Tucker's side, Ella kneels and puts her face close to Tucker's. She begins unbuttoning the top buttons of Tucker's shirt. "What's happening?"

In a hoarse whisper, Tucker says, "It'll pass. I'm jest havin' a spell. Help me get t' th' shade by th' barn."

Tucker gets to one knee. Ella puts Tucker's arm over her shoulder and begins lifting. Slowly, Tucker rises. With Ella's help, she walks unsteadily to the side of the barn and leans back against it. Ella joins her in the shade.

Breathing heavily from the exertion, Ella says, "What kind of spells are you talking about? How long has this been going on?"

"It ain't nothin'," Tucker says. "It'll ease up in a minute."

Concern digs a furrow between Ella's eyes.

Lifting her head, Tucker takes a long, deep breath. "Now that's better," she says. "Y' know, I've gotta tell th' kids 'bout their mama."

"Oh shit," Ella says. Her face immediately reddens. "I'm sorry. I didn't mean to say that. I meant to say, 'Oh shoot.'"

Through her dried tears, Tucker manages a half-smile. "Woman, y' ain't gotta 'pologize t' me fer that."

Ella smiles briefly, then says, "The kids....Do you want me to go get April and bring her up here so you can tell all of them at the same time?"

"I reckon so," Tucker replies. "I'll mee'chu up at th' house."

With a look of unease, Ella says, "Are you going to be okay to walk?"

Standing erect and breathing easily, Tucker says, "Sure, I'll be fine." She lumbers toward her house while Ella walks quickly to her own.

Seeing Tucker coming into the yard, August and March come out of the house onto the porch.

"What did the sheriff want?" August calls out to the approaching Tucker.

"Yeah," March adds, "what's going on? I saw Ella come up there, too."

Ignoring the boys, Tucker walks past the porch. "Ya'll come t' th' backyard. Let's sit under th' shade tree fer a bit."

August and March share puzzled expressions, raise their shoulders, and follow Tucker's trail.

Catching up with Tucker, March says, "The sheriff sure was hot and sweaty. Where had he been? Why did he come out here? Was he looking for somebody? Are we in trouble, or something? I promise I haven't been in trouble in school or the bus either."

Arriving under the welcoming shade of the giant oak tree, Tucker walks to the trunk where a five gallon bucket lies on its side. Turning it upside down, she sits on the bottom and leans back against the tree. "You boys jes' have a seat. Yore sister, April's, comin', too."

March glances quickly at August. August scowls at him and motions for him to sit in the grass. They try to read Tucker's placid expression, but find nothing helpful there.

The sound of frantic cicadas, eager to enjoy their brief life in the sun, fills the summer air. August picks up a nearby stick and idly digs a hole. March repeatedly tries to catch a tassel fly as it hovers close by.

In a few moments the three of them hear the sounds of

approaching feet. Looking, they see Ella and April approaching hand in hand.

Letting go of Ella's hand and looking frightened, April runs to Tucker's side. "What's wrong?" April asks. "Ella wouldn't tell me."

Overlooking the question, Tucker puts her hand on April's head. "Why don'chu sit down with yore brothers. We gotta talk."

Sitting cross-legged in a semi-circle, the three children look attentively at Tucker. Ella takes a seat on the ground behind them.

"I got somethin' t' tell y'," Tucker begins.

"Is it about the sheriff?" March interrupts.

August punches him on the shoulder. "Will you just shut up and let Tucker tell us?!"

Rubbing his shoulder, March looks chagrined and returns his focus to Tucker.

"It's 'bout yore mama," Tucker says.

A quietness blankets the small group under the tree that is so suffocating, that even the cicadas pause their incessant chatter to listen.

Coughing to clear her throat, Tucker takes her thick, scratched glasses off her face and holds them in her hand.

Ella is started to realize she's never seen the color of Tucker's eyes and is amazed at their beautiful bright green hue.

Tucker looks into the distance and says, "The sheriff told us she's dead."

August's mouth drops open. March's eyes fill with tears. April's expression does not change. Ella's eyes redden.

Burying his face in his lap, March cries out, "Mama!"

In a voice that sounds detached from him, August says, "Mama's dead?"

Looking back at Ella, April's expression asks for permission to join her.

Moving on her all-fours, Ella gets close enough to the children to reach her arms around them. "I'm so sorry children, so very sorry."

Ella's touch breaks the cord that had tethered August's tears to his heart. As he begins crying, he says, "What happened? I mean, how did she die?"

Ella winces when Tucker says, "The sheriff tol'us somebody killt 'er."

Jumping to his fist with clinched fists, Augusts yells, "Who did it? I'll kill 'em! Nobody's gonna do that to my mama and get away with it. I'll kill 'em."

Ella cuts in, "There's still lots that we don't know yet. The sheriff said there will be an investigation to figure out exactly what happened. So, we need to wait until we get more information before we can tell you all anything else. Why don't we go in the house and make us something to eat?"

Standing, she reaches for April and August's hands. "Come on, let's go inside."

April readily takes her hand. August takes her other hand and reaches for March. "Come on March," he says. March takes August's hand and stands.

Turning to Tucker, Ella sees her staring toward some faraway place. "What about you Tucker? You want join us?"

When Tucker doesn't acknowledge her, Ella says to the children, "You all come with me. Let's let Tucker rest out here for awhile."

FOR TUCKER

Chapter Fifteen

Ella, wearing a black dress and hat, opens the back door of her car and April gets in. Ella reaches in and smoothes the wrinkles out of April's navy dress. "You look nice," she says.

Smiling, April says, "So do you."

They drive in silence the few hundred yards to Tucker's house. As they pull in the yard, March comes out of the house, his dark hair parted on one side and plastered to his head. August appears in the doorway. His normally unruly hair has been picked into a perfectly round fro.

Rolling down her window, Ella calls out, "You boys come on and get in the back seat with your sister."

After the boys are loaded, Ella turns the car around and heads toward town.

"What's going to happen at this thing called a foorel?" March asks.

"I keep telling you," August chastises, "it's a fun-er-al, not a foorel."

Looking in her rearview mirror at the boys, Ella says, "It's just a chance to share some memories about a person who has died. There'll be a preacher who will say a few words. And there will be some pretty music."

"Like Three Dog Night?" March laughs.

August punches him and says, "You really are a fool, you know it? Can't you be serious for mama?"

March shoots August an angry look, but says nothing.

Ella says, "Let's just all ride quietly to the funeral home."

Though quiet on the outside, Ella's mind is in a whirl, trying to process all that has happened and all she has learned in the last thirty-six hours.

It began when she asked Tucker if she wanted Ella to try and contact Maisy's father about her death.

"Ain't no need t' try that," Tucker replies. "He's done met his Maker a long time ago."

"I've never heard you talk about your father," Ella gently probes.

"M' father was a sorry son of a bitch. He abused me all m' life, up 'til th' day I kilt 'im."

Ella feels herself stagger in reaction to this unexpected bombshell. She has no time to recover before Tucker drops a bigger bomb.

"An' he was Maisy's father, too."

Ella stares at Tucker.

"It's a helluva note, ain't it?" Tucker says. "Don't nobody livin' know 'bout all that. You's th' onliest one."

"I....I don't know what to say," Ella says. "I figured you had a hard time growing up. But I never dreamed.....," her voice chokes as tears well up.

"It ain't nothing. 'twas a long time ago."

"How come Tucker didn't come home last night?" August's question snaps Ella back to the present.

She glances at him in the rearview mirror. "She spent the night at the funeral home. That's the way everybody did years ago. Someone would stay all night with the body of their loved one."

"That's scary," April says.

Pulling up to the front of the funeral home, Ella stops the car.

"Okay now, everyone follow me and mind your manners."

The sound of taped organ music greets the four of them as they open the front door. Ella leads the way to the parlor room where the service will be held. The room is empty except for Tucker, Smiley Carter, Shady Green, Mary Beth Chandler, and the preacher.

Ella ushers the children into the empty chairs beside Tucker.

The music fades out and the preacher walks to the podium.

"When I moved here twenty years ago," he begins, "it wasn't long before I began hearing about Tucker and her daughter, Maisy. Most of what I heard was not worth listening to because it was nothing more than gossip. And gossip is a damnable sin."

Looking directly at Tucker he says, "So I decided I would go see for myself what all the talk was about." Smiling, he says, "Do you remember my first visit to your place, Tucker?"

Tucker's stony expression is inscrutable.

"Well I do," the preacher says. "Tucker was shelling corn off the cob for her hogs. When I introduced myself and stuck out my hand to shake hers, she stuck an ear of corn in my hand and said, "Git busy.""

Shady Green cackles, "Tha' be her aw'wight."

Smiley Carter concurs with Shady by giving a hearty "amen."

The preacher continues, "I've visited Tucker many times over the past twenty years, a detail that I'm sure would shock my parishioners. I visited because I found Tucker refreshing. I never had to guess where I stood with Tucker."

Shifting his gaze to the small audience, he says, "Maisy was a different matter, though. She never seemed content. She was restless. And I'd say that restlessness was her undoing.

"For those of you left behind, it will be difficult for you to fit

Maisy's violent death into your heart in a way that will make sense, for there's no sense to be made of it."

Pulling out a white handkerchief, he wipes the sweat off his face. "To you children, I will say I am sorry that you didn't get to live long enough to experience the effects of the reformed life that I so badly wanted your mother to achieve.

"And to you, Tucker, I will say I regret that you have another sorrow to add to your difficult life. But this one thing I know – there is a better life awaiting us all. In that sweet bye and bye all our burdens will be lifted and all our sorrows will be washed away. In heaven there'll be no weeping nor pining. May we all eagerly look forward to that day."

As the preacher leaves the podium, Smiley Carter rises, walks a few steps past the family, then turns to face them. All eyes are fixed on him.

The organ music begins playing again. After the introduction plays, Smiley Carter opens his mouth and, in a baritone voice reminiscent of Johnny Hartman, sings,

Well, I'm tired and so weary, but I must go along;

Till the Lord comes and calls me away, oh, yes;

Well the morning is bright, and the Lamb is the Light;

And the night, night is as fair as the day, oh, yes.

There will be peace in the valley for me some day;

There will be peace in the valley for me, O Lord, I pray;

There'll be no sadness, no sorrow, no trouble I'll see;

There will be peace in the valley for me.

There the flowers will be blooming, and the grass will be green;

And the skies will be clear and serene, oh, yes;

Well the sun ever beams, in this valley of dreams;

And no clouds there will ever be seen, oh, yes.

There will be peace in the valley for me some day;

There will be peace in the valley for me, O Lord, I pray;

There'll be no sadness, no sorrow, no trouble I'll see;

There will be peace in the valley for me.

Well, the bear will be gentle, and the wolf will be tame;

And the lion shall lay down by the lamb, oh, yes;

Well the beast from the wild, shall be led by a little child;

And I'll be changed, changed from the creature that I am, oh, yes.

There will be peace in the valley for me some day;

There will be peace in the valley for me, O Lord, I pray;

There'll be no sadness, no sorrow, no trouble I'll see;

There will be peace in the valley for me.

As the last notes settle on the hearts of the audience, the only sound heard is sniffling. Everyone is wiping tears, except Tucker.

Her face a deep crimson, Tucker sits stiffly, her arms folded across her chest.

Ted Mays, the funeral director, comes into the room and announces, "This concludes the service for Maisy. Because her body is still at the coroner's in Memphis, there will not be an internment at this time. Thank you all for coming."

Outside, Tucker and the children pile into Ella's car. After speaking to the preacher, Shady Green, Smiley Carter and Mary Beth, Ella gets in the driver's seat.

They ride in silence as they pass through town and head toward their houses. As they turn onto the road that will take them home, Tucker says, "Somebody's gonna pay fer what happened t' Maisy. Somebody's gonna pay."

~~~~~~~~~~~~~~~~~

Chapter Sixteen

Two days after Maisy's funeral Sheriff Ron Harris eases his police cruiser down the dirt lane. Parking beside the Rescue Squad's truck, he gets out and puts on his Stetson hat. He walks toward the Obion river, passing several other patrol cars, and joins the group of officers and volunteers awaiting him.

A white headed deputy, whose belly makes it impossible to know if his pants are held up by a belt, steps from the circle and says, "Come this way sheriff." Turning, he leads the sheriff to a boat that is pulled up on the bank.

Pointing to two wet, mud-covered men, the deputy says, "Joey and Carl are the ones who found it."

The four men gather on either side of the boat. Peering in, the sheriff sees what has prompted the radio call for him to come out and inspect the discovery for himself – a whitened skull.

Looking at Joey and Carl, the sheriff asks, "And where did you find it?"

Joey and Carl look at each other and then Joey says, "It was in that patch of lily pads where Maisy's body was found. We were looking for any sort of evidence that might help us find out who murdered her, just like you ordered us to."

"We didn't know what it was at first," Carl adds. "It was covered in mud and moss."

Shifting his toothpick to the corner of his mouth, the sheriff asks, "What about any other bones? A skull doesn't just appear out of thin air and not have the rest of the skeleton attached. Did you look for more bones?"

Joey shifts his feet nervously. "That mud out there must be ten inches deep or more in places. Nearly anything on the bottom just disappears over time. It's a miracle we found that skull."

Fixing them with a hard stare, the sheriff says, "That didn't answer my question. Did you look for more bones?"

"We did for a little bit," Carl says. "But all we found were sticks that we thought might be bones."

Hoping to vouch for Carl and Joey, the deputy says, "You'd just about have to drain that slough and let it dry for a month before you could know exactly what's in there."

Stepping into the boat, the sheriff squats beside the skull to get a better look. Without taking his eyes off the skull, he says, "I guess you're right. You boys did a good job.

"I'd say this is definitely the skull of an adult. And I'd say it's been out there for a very long time."

Standing up, he makes a sweeping motion with his arm. "But what are the odds of finding evidence of two possible murders in the same place out here in the middle of nowhere?"

Pointing to the deputy, he says, "Jessie, bag that thing, put it in my car and wait for me there." Raising his voice, he calls out, "All you men gather around here for a minute."

Once the deputies and volunteer rescue workers are around him, the sheriff says, "Now I want every one of you to listen very closely to what I'm about to say. I don't want one word to leak out about this skull Carl and Joey found. I mean not one peep. And if something does leak out, somebody's going to have to answer to me. Everybody understand?"

There is a general murmur of agreement from the men.

"Good," the sheriff says. "All of you worked really hard the past several days. Good work. We're through out here now. Load everything up and head back to town."

Getting into his squad car, the sheriff cranks his engine and turns the air conditioner on high. He and Jessie sit in silence as, one by one, the other emergency vehicles leave.

When the last one leaves, Jessie says, "What's on your mind

sheriff?"

"How old are you, Jessie?"

Laughing, Jessie replies, "I'm as old as that mud that Carl and Joey had smeared on them."

"No, I'm serious," the sheriff says.

"Well, this November I'll be seventy years old."

"That's about what I thought. And how long have you been in law enforcement?"

"Including my time in the military, it's been about fifty years."

Putting the car in gear, the sheriff slowly pulls onto the highway and heads toward town. Jessie lights a cigarette and lowers his window a bit to let the smoke escape.

After several minutes of silence, Jessie breaks in, "I can hear your wheels turning, but I don't know what you're thinking."

"Okay," the sheriff begins, "let me ask you a question. What's this skull got to do with Maisy Tucker?"

"I don't know. Maybe something. Maybe nothing. It's hard to tell."

"Look," the sheriff snaps, "I'm not a lawyer trying to trap you. Just answer my question with a straight answer."

Flipping his cigarette out the window, Jessie says, "I remember when your granddaddy was sheriff. He always said there wasn't no such thing as coincidence."

"Exactly what I was thinking," the sheriff cuts in.

"So let me tell you a story," Jessie says. "Suppose there was this man who had a daughter. This man was known to be a very rough sort of feller, kept to himself – a real surly character. And let's suppose that anytime someone saw his daughter she looked like a whipped pup. Maybe there was rumors going around that this man was abusing his daughter, and I don't mean just physically."

Jessie pauses to light another cigarette.

"Give me one of those," the sheriff says. "I swear, every time I try to quit smoking, something happens to set me off again."

Smiling, Jessie offers him the pack.

After they light up their cigarettes, Jessie continues, "Let's suppose that every man in the county would just like to have an excuse to get rid of this vermin of a man, but no one can ever unbottle the truth. And what if, when this little girl is about sixteen years old, suddenly nobody ever sees this man anymore. He don't come to town, never is seen in his field – I mean it's like he vanished into thin air. Some people might say that the fellow ran off because he was afraid someone was going to find out what was going on between him and his girl."

The sheriff's eyes narrow as he listens intently to Jessie's story. The muscles in his jaw flex repeatedly. Glancing at Jessie, he says, "Are you saying somebody caught him out one night and did him in?"

"May have happened that way," Jessie says. "But suppose, just suppose, that this girl finally got her fill of his evil ways. And maybe she figures out a way to kill him – "

The sheriff's eyes widen and he takes his foot off the accelerator. "And she dumps the body out here in the swamp! Do you mean Tucker killed – "

"I don't mean anything," Jessie cuts in. "I'm just speaking in suppositions. It's all speculation." He turns in the car seat until he is facing the sheriff. "But I'll tell you what your granddaddy said about this very story a long time ago. He said sometimes a person gets what they deserve, even if it is outside the law."

~~~~~~~~~~~~~~~

DAVID JOHNSON

Chapter Seventeen

Sheriff Ron Harris pulls to a stop in front of Maisy's apartment. He walks past the T.B.I. car and another black sedan in the driveway. Opening the front door, he steps inside where one man is putting his camera away and two technicians are closing their briefcases.

District Attorney, Whalen Kennedy, who played football with Ron in high school, is also present. Stepping toward the sheriff and sticking out a hand, he says, "Hey Ron. How's it going? Sure is hot out there, isn't it?"

Shaking Whalen's hand, the sheriff says, "It's summer time in west Tennessee, that's what it is. H H H – hot, hazy and humid. What have they found in here?"

"They say it was definitely wiped down. There are two drink glasses, but only one has fingerprints on it – Maisy's. Even the bottle's been wiped down."

"You and your investigator had already concluded it must have been someone she knew since there were no indications of a struggle. Nothing was taken, as far as we can tell. Fresh sheets were on the bed, so no chance of getting any evidence there."

Glancing around the apartment, the sheriff says, "It'd be nice if we had at least a sliver of something to go on."

The T.B.I. agents line up to leave the apartment. One of them says, "This is our second time to sweep the apartment and we didn't find anything new. Sorry."

Whalen shakes his hand and says, "Thanks fellows. We appreciate the extra effort."

As the agents walk out the door, the last man pauses, looking at the wall behind the door. Letting go of the door, he steps to the wall, putting his face inches from the surface. "Hey Turner," he calls out. "Get back in here a second."

The sheriff and Whalen exchange a glance. "What it is it?" Whalen asks.

"Maybe nothing," the agent replies.

Turner comes back in and seeing his fellow agent with his face against a wall, says, "Find something Johnny?"

"Bring me the fingerprint kit," Johnny replies.

Turner sits the black briefcase on the floor by Johnny. Without moving his face from the wall, Johnny says, "Hand me the brush. I don't want to take my eyes off this."

Turner fills the fine hairs of the brush with Cyanoacrylate and carefully hands it to him.

Johnny carefully spins the brush across an area on the wall and steps back. After waiting a couple of minutes, he places a black gelatin lifter over the area and then peels it off.

Holding it up to the overhead light, he says, "That's nice."

"What've you got?" the sheriff asks impatiently.

"Looks like someone put their hand against the wall," Johnny says. "And it's definitely larger than Maisy's hand."

"Finally!" the sheriff and Whalen exclaim simultaneously.

"Maybe this is the break we've been looking for," Whalen says.

"So, how long before we know if there's a match anywhere?" the sheriff asks.

"Hard to tell," Johnny answers. "Sometimes a week, sometimes a month. Since it's a murder case, it'll have top priority. We'll do our best."

"The only problem," the sheriff says, "is that lots of men have been in her apartment. So there's no telling when that print was made or who it will match."

Nodding agreement, Whalen says, "That's for certain."

Outside the apartment a gray Oldsmobile Cutlass pulls in behind the sheriff's car. The driver nervously licks his lips, then opens the door and gets out.

On legs that feel like jell-o, he slowly walks past the T.B.I. car and his boss's car. Walking up the steps to the front door of the apartment, he is startled when Johnny opens the door and bustles past him.

Stepping into the living room, he says, "Hey boss. Hey sheriff. What's the latest?"

Whalen says, "We may have finally gotten a break. They found a full handprint on the wall. And they're certain it isn't Maisy's."

The sheriff looks at him and says, "Are you okay? You look pale as a sheet."

With a wave of his hand, he replies, "Sure, sure, I'm alright. I've just had a touch of a stomach bug."

"Listen," Whalen says, "why don't you go with the T.B.I. guys back to our office and help them clear out their stuff? They'll be heading back to Memphis."

"Sure thing boss," he says. Turning around unsteadily, he makes his way back to his car.

Sitting behind the steering wheel, he tries to calm his breathing. He tries to retrace in his mind every step he made the night he was in Maisy's apartment. As he visualizes the events of the evening, he suddenly remembers staggering when he picked Maisy up off the floor and planting his hand on the wall to catch his balance.

His face flushes and he gasps. "Damn!" he says. "Oh my God what am I going to do?!"

Reaching for his collar, he loosens his tie and unbuttons the top button of his shirt. Slowly he lowers his forehead to the steering wheel.

Inside the apartment, the sheriff nods his head toward the street and says, "How's that kid working out in your office?"

"Not too bad," Whalen replies. "His biggest problem is who his dad is. He has the same entitled attitude that grates on me. Thinks he knows everything when he really doesn't, if you know what I mean. Plus he has a roving eye for women."

"Sounds to me like he's a lot of trouble," the sheriff says.

As they walk outside, Whalen says, "He's got a sharp legal mind and a good eye for detail. And he's ambitious. I use those two traits to my advantage."

They both look up and watch as the gray Cutlass pulls away from the curb and heads toward town.

"I'll probably see you tomorrow," Whalen says to the sheriff.

"Let me know the minute you learn something about the print," the sheriff says.

"Will do."

"One more thing," the sheriff adds, "have you ever heard the expression, 'Sometimes a person gets what they deserve, even if it is outside the law'?"

Cocking his head, Whalen says, "That's a curious thing for you to say. What's going on?"

"You lawyers!" the sheriff says in exasperation. "Can't you just answer a question?!"

"Okay, okay," Whalen says. "I didn't mean to rile you up. Sure I've heard that expression before."

"And do you believe it's true?"

"Just between me and you?"

"Yes," the sheriff says, "just between me and you."

"Then I'd have to say yes, it is true. Now, you've got to tell me what prompted all this."

Shaking his head, the sheriff replies, "It's nothing. I've just been chasing random thoughts lately. You have a good evening."

~~~~~~~~~~~~~~~~~~~~~~

Chapter Eighteen

Tucker pushes the bushel basket ahead a few feet with her foot. Lifting the dark green leaves of the purple hull pea vines, she reaches for a handful of foot-long pea pods and pulls them from the plant. She pitches them into the bushel basket. All of this while remaining bent at the waist at a ninety degree angle.

Sweat drips from the end of her nose as she nears the end of the row. Once there, she slowly straightens and seeks shelter in the shade of a sassafras tree.

The sound of an engine draws her attention to the road. Driving up her road is Smiley Carter on his Ford tractor.

She watches as he drives right up to her front porch where the boys are shelling peas. They both answer an unheard question by pointing toward the garden. Carter waves a thank you to them and heads toward the garden.

Stopping when he gets to the garden gate, Carter shuts off his tractor and unfolds his large frame from the seat. Closing the gate behind him as he enters the garden area, he scans the garden until he catches sight of Tucker under the tree.

Throwing one of his large hands into the air, he strides toward her.

As he gets close, he winks at Tucker and says, "Mmm mmmm, them is some fine lookin' peas. Must'a had somethin' to do with how the ground was plowed."

Tucker does not reply.

Sensing her somber mood, Carter looks more closely at her. "You's got the sadness, Tucker. Yes you does. An' you gots ever right to the sadness. Losin' a child......." His voice drifts off.

Turning her head away from him, Tucker spits tobacco juice. Looking at Carter, she says, "That was a kind thing y' done, singin' at Maisy's fun'ral. Thanks."

Shaking his head, Carter says, "'T'weren't nothin' Tucker. It was the least I could do."

"An' I didn' know y' had such a good singin' voice. Y' sounded like somethin' off th' radio."

Carter smiles. "Thank you, thank you. I do loves to sing."

There is a pause in their conversation. Carter shifts from one foot to the other. He takes out his handkerchief and blows his nose. "Yes sir, them's some fine lookin' peas."

"What'n th' world's wrong with you?" Tucker asks. "Y' act as nervous as a long tail cat in a room full o' rockin' chairs. I know y' didn't come 'ere t' talk 'bout my peas. What's on yore mind?"

Licking his lips before speaking, Carter asks, "Has the sheriff got any leads yet on who killed Maisy?"

"None that'es shared w' me. It's been a week since th' fun'ral an' I ain't heerd nothin' from 'im. You git t' town more 'an me. Whata you hear?"

"Rumors," Carter replies, "nothin' but rumors. There's for sure been no arrests. I seen a T.B.I. car at Maisy's last week. Must be doing fingerprint stuff."

Looking at her again, he adds, "How you holding up, Tucker?"

"If'n I kin git m' hands on whoever murdered Maisy, I'll be jest fine," Tucker answers.

Just as Carter is about to speak, Tucker continues, "Look, I know what kinda person Maisy was. I ain't stupid. But not even a dog deserves t' have done what was done t' 'er."

When Carter doesn't say anything, she says, "Don'chu agree w' me? Or do y' think she deserved what she got?"

Seeming startled, Carter says, "No...yes...I mean no. I mean nobody deserves what she got."

Tucker cocks her head to one side as she looks at Carter.

He sees her curiosity and unspoken question. "Okay, I gots something to tells you Tucker. And it's something big, something important. But I's scared to tell, cause it may mean something and it may mean nothing."

He feels her eyes piercing him from behind her nearly opaque glasses.

"Well here's how it is," he begins. "You know I likes to night fish, 'specially along the Obion. Well about four months ago I was fishing north of Latham; fishing under the bridge. I was the only one there that night. I wasn't catching much, but I was enjoying the quiet.

"About midnight I heard a car slowing down. The headlights swept down the road bank as it turned down the dirt lane where people unload their boats.

"The headlights were low to the ground, so I figured it was a car. 'Some kids come out her to go parking,' I said to myself.

"This fellow gets out of the car and shines a flashlight. I was under the bridge on the other side of the river. I didn't have no lantern burning, so he never knew I was there.

"He starts walking along the bank, shining his flashlight like he's looking for something. He disappears into the timber and is gone about fifteen minutes when I hear an engine start. Sounds like a lawnmower engine. So I figure it must be a Reelfoot boat.

"Sure enough, in a minute here he comes in that Reelfoot boat and runs it up on the bank behind his car.

"He opens the trunk of his car and gets something out, something really heavy. He has it across his shoulder, like it's a big feed sack or something."

Carter notices Tucker's breath becoming more rapid and her

nostrils flaring. He glances away and continues. "Now remember, it was dark. Even though it was a full moon, the cloud cover kept everything mostly hidden. Shapes was easy to see, but details was hard.

"This man dumps whatever it is over his shoulder into the boat, pushes out into the water, starts the boat motor and heads back into the timber."

Carter feels his own breath quickening. His mouth feels like it has cotton in it. "Where's your water jar?" he asks.

Tucker points to a spot at the base of the tree. "Help yoreself."

After gulping several swallows, Carter continues. "This fella goes so far that I soon can't hear the engine. He's gone for maybe an hour and I hear the engine coming back my way.

"He runs the boat ashore and gets out. He walks to his car and opens the door to get in. That's when there's a sudden break in the clouds. That full moon lights things up like it's midday.

"The man looks up at the moon and I get a real good look at him. And I realize I've seen him before, but I can't remember where. And I can't remember what his name is.

"Now remember, Tucker, this was nearly five months ago. I done forgot all about it until they found Maisy's body. And I started trying to remember who the fellow was that I saw.

"It was at Maisy's funeral that I suddenly remembered."

Pausing and looks directly at Tucker, Carter says, "It was Judge Jack's and Miss Ella's boy, Cade."

Tucker' mouth drops open. She sways back and forth. Her knees suddenly buckle and she crumples to the ground.

~~~~~~~~~~~~~~~~~

Chapter Nineteen

Kneeling beside Tucker's inert body, Smiley Carter frantically calls her name, "Tucker! Tucker! Lord almighty, Tucker, wake up!"

He looks in every direction in hopes of seeing someone he can call to. Seeing no one, he lifts her hand and begins patting it.

Tucker emits a low moan.

"That's it," Carter says, "come on now, you's gonna be alright."

When Tucker stirs, he gets behind her and puts his hands under her arms. "Let me help you sit up."

Once in a sitting position, Tucker takes off her glasses and vigorously rubs her face. Giving her had a energetic shake, she says, "What happened?"

Putting her glasses back on, she looks at Carter and says, "Oh, now I 'member."

Folding his long legs and sitting cross-legged in front of her, Carter says, "They just wasn't no easy way to tell you, Tucker. It was a shock to me, too, when I figured out who I seen that night."

"How come y' ain't tol' this t' the sheriff?"

"Well, this here's the problem," Carter replies. "That night the man was is such a hurry to leave that he left his boat on the bank of the river. I mean, he just drove off and left it. So I waited awhile to see if he'd come back. When he didn't, I took the boat for myself. I ain't never had a Reelfoot boat and you know I likes to fish.

"I ain't said nothing to nobody 'cause I was afraid they'd find out I took the boat and they'd arrest me."

Tucker's eyes open and close rapidly as she processes all that Carter has told her. "Judge Jack's boy," she says slowly. After a pause, she adds, "And Miss Ella's." She shakes her head. "Oh my lord, my lord...." She closes her eyes.

"Yes," Carter says solemnly. "As Mama Mattie would say, 'It shore 'nuff is a mess.'"

As they sit in contemplative silence, the singing of cicadas and field larks fills the void.

Reaching toward Carter, Tucker says, "Help me up."

With a grunt, Carter stands. Grasping Tuckers hand firmly in his, he pulls. They both groan with the effort until, finally, Tucker is standing.

"Sometimes," Tucker says, "I git tired o' fightin' against life. Seems like it's always somethin'."

Carter cocks his head to one side. "'Tis so, 'tis so Tucker. But what're we gonna do?"

"Y' sound scared," Tucker says. "I ain't never knowed y' t' be scared o' nothin'. What's got in t' y'?"

"It's Judge Jack," Carter says. "That's what I'm worried about. He runs this county. What he says goes. He'll find a way to put me in prison afore he lets his boy get in trouble."

"Ain't but one thing t' do," Tucker says. "I gotta go see Ella. She'll know what's best."

As she begins walking toward the garden gate, Carter says, "Let me carry you on my tractor to her house. You don't needs to be walking after your faintin' spell."

When they get to his tractor, Tucker eyes it skeptically. "An' where am I supposed t' ride? There ain't but one seat."

Pointing to the rear axle, Carter says, "Climb up here and put your feet there. Then you can sit on the rear wheel fender. Gimme your hand and I'll help you."

Once Tucker is in place, Carter cranks the tractor, eases out on the clutch and makes his way to Ella's. When they arrive, Carter helps Tucker off the tractor.

As Carter starts to remount the tractor, Tucker says, "Where y' think you're goin'? Git down off'n there. You're comin' in, too."

Giving no room for discussion, she turns and strides toward Ella's front door. Reluctantly, Carter follows.

Tucker strikes Ella's door twice and waits.

When the door opens, Ella's face registers surprise. Before she can invite them in, Tucker walks past her.

"We come t' talk t' you," Tucker says.

Taking his cap off, Carter nods at Ella as he walks past.

Ella closes the door and turns to face them. She has learned it is impossible to read Tucker's expression and body language, so she waits.

Tucker shifts from one foot to the other. Carter focuses his attention on the floor.

Finally, Tucker says, "Maybe we could sit 'round yore table n' talk."

"Sure we can," Ella says. She leads the way to her dining room. "Coffee or tea, either one of you?"

Pulling out a chair to sit, Carter looks at her and says, "Some iced tea sure would be nice. My throat's as dry as sand. And bring some for Tucker, too. She had a spell a bit ago and needs to drink something."

A look of concern halts Ella's steps to the kitchen. She turns to look closely at Tucker. "A spell? What sort of spell?"

"I'm fine," Tucker replies. "We'll git t' all that inna minute."

A quizzical expression appears on Ella's face, but she refrains from asking more questions. Proceeding to the kitchen, she fixes everyone some iced tea and brings it to the table.

Once she sits down, she looks expectantly toward Tucker.

Taking a deep breath, Tucker begins, "This here ain't gonna be easy. I ain't even sure you's th' one I oughta be talkin' to 'bout this. But I ain't got nobody else t' turn to."

Ella frowns. "Is this about April?"

Looking surprised, Tucker says, "Oh no. It ain't got nothin' t' do with her. It's about Maisy."

Ella notices Carter squeezing his cap and his furtive glance from Tucker to her. "Have they found the killer?" she asks.

"I ain't heard it, if'n they did," Tucker replies. "This is about somthin' Carter seen back in February." She pauses and looks at Carter. "Why don't y' just tell 'er what y' tol' me."

Holding his twisted cap between his legs, Carter looks at Ella and says, "Well here's what happened...."

When Ella finishes listening to Smiley Carter's tale about the fateful February night and his realization later of the identity of the person he saw, she stares toward Carter but her eyes are unfocused. Her complexion is ashen. She mouths Cade's name but makes no sound.

Tucker eases her thick, rough hand across the table toward Ella. Ella looks down at it and then up at Tucker. A look of horror seizes her face. In a whisper, she says, "Oh no," and begins shaking her head.

Ignoring Tucker's hand, Ella gets up from the table and begins pacing. "No, no, no," she says. "There must be a mistake." Looking at Carter, she says, "You said yourself that it was dark that night. How can you be so certain it was Cade? How well can a person see, even with the full moon, at such a distance?"

Dropping his head, Carter says, "I'm sorry Miss Ella, but I know what I seen. And even though the rest of me is getting old, Doc White says I've got the eyesight of a twenty year old."

"But you don't know what he put in the boat," Ella says. "You didn't see what it was, did you?"

"No ma'am. I didn't see that. Didn't really pay much attention because I figured it was somebody doing some fishing. But I knew it was odd for someone to come there pulling a boat behind a car."

Ella begins pacing again. "But what would Cade be doing with Maisy? Why in the world would he want to hurt her? Maisy was nothing but a - - "

She stops in mid-sentence and looks at Tucker. "Oh Tucker," she says in a pleading tone, "I'm sorry. I didn't mean to say anything hurtful. I'm just rambling. Please forgive me."

Folding her arms across her chest, Tucker says, "Y' ain't got nothin' t' 'pologize fer. I know what Maisy was. But nobody deserved what happened t' her."

Ella clasps both hands to her mouth. Rushing back to sit in her chair at the table, she leans on her elbows toward Tucker. Her voice trembles as she says, "Tucker, please hear me. The biggest tragedy here is that your daughter, your only child, suffered an awful death. I sincerely and deeply regret that."

As she is speaking, Tucker's face begins to redden and tears well up.

"And now," Ella continues, "I've learned there is a possibility that my only child may have been responsible for the murder. But why?" Tears begin streaming down her cheeks.

Tucker unfolds her arms and places her hands over Ella's, dwarfing them. She begins to cry and lowers her head onto her forearms.

Ella mirrors Tucker's movements and washes her own forearms in tears.

The tops of their heads touch in the middle of the table.

Himself moved, Carter places a hand on each woman's head and says softly, "The Lord is my shepherd, I shall not want. He maketh me to lie down in green pastures. He leadeth me beside the still waters. He restoreth my soul......."

~~~~~~~~~~~~~~~~~~~~

Chapter Twenty

Throwing his head back, Cade McDade punctuates the air with a hearty laugh. The other men at the table join him in laughter.

"That's the best one yet," Cade says to the man on his right. "Where do you find all your jokes?"

Before the man can answer, Cade yells to a passing waitress, "Hey sweet thing, bring another round of drinks for us, won't you?"

The waitress flashes a white smile and winks. "Anything for you Cade," she says.

This prompts a chorus of whistles and catcalls from the group of men. "You better get you some of that," one of them says to Cade.

"Who says he hasn't already?" another one laughs.

Another round of laughter erupts.

Shaking his head, Cade says, "No, no boys. Not anymore. I'm reformed. It's time for me to settle down. All of your all's lies about me through the years have given me a reputation that's hard to live up to and to live down."

The group is silent for a moment until, as if on cue, they simultaneously burst out laughing.

"That's a good one, Cade," one of them says.

"Reformed my ass," another one scoffs.

Suddenly everyone's attention swings toward the figure of the approaching waitress with her tray of drinks. As she sets the tray on their table, Cade hands her a twenty dollar bill. Placing it slowly in the cleavage of her breasts, she says to Cade, "Anything else?"

"No thanks Tiffany," Cade says. "We'll be fine."

Looking back at the faces of his friends at the table, Cade reads the skepticism in their expressions. Picking up his glass, he takes a big gulp and stands. Waving a dismissive hand toward them, he says, "You guys go ahead and believe what you want. I'm going home to my wife."

As he walks away, the covert accusations of his friends, wearing the disguise of teases, echo across the room and close the door behind him as he steps outside. Finding his gray Cutlass, he opens the door and slides inside.

Driving past the court house on his way home, he recognizes the car of Whalen Kennedy sitting under the street light. He looks to the third floor and sees lights on in their suite of offices.

Turning on his blinker, he decides to circle the square. On the opposite side of the court house he sees the patrol car of Sheriff Ron Harris and beside it a car with a T.B.I. logo on the door.

A bead of sweat appears above Cade's upper lip. His hands clench and unclench around the steering wheel. He glances in the rear view mirror.

Proceeding to his house, he forces himself to breathe slowly.

Walking in the back door, he calls out, "I'm home Julie."

From deeper within the house, a woman's voice answers, "Hi Cade. I'm in here. But you need to call Whalen first. He called earlier and asked me to have you call him as soon as you got home."

Keeping his voice light, he says, "Did he say what it was about?"

"No. He just said it was important."

Lifting the receiver off the wall phone, Cade dials the number from memory.

After the first ring, his boss answers, "Kennedy here."

"Hey Whalen, this is Cade. Julie asked me to call you. What's up?"

"It's the Maisy Tucker case. The T.B.I. found a match on some prints. Can you come to the office?"

"Uh, you mean tonight? Now?"

"That's exactly what I mean," Whalen snaps.

Whalen's tone is so sharp that Cade jerks the receiver from his ear. Slowly bringing it back to his face, he says, "Well sure I can. No problem. I'll be there in a couple of minutes."

Hanging up the phone, he is startled by Julie's voice beside him.

"Is something wrong?" she asks. "You're white as a sheet. And why are you so jumpy?"

"No, nothing's wrong," he replies. "It's just that you snuck up on me. I've got to go to the office. There's been a break in one of our cases."

Walking up the marble steps of the court house, Cade's leather soled shoes echo throughout the empty building. His sweating palm squeaks as he slides it up the hand rail. He quickly wipes both palms on his pants.

Arriving at the third floor, he turns down the darkened hallway to a door with light sneaking out at the bottom. Taking a deep breath, he opens the door and steps inside.

The electricity in the air makes the hair on the back of his neck stand at attention. The three men in the room turn to look at him: Whalen is standing by the window behind his desk; sheriff Harris is sitting at one end of the desk and putting out his cigarette; the third man, sitting at the opposite end of the desk, Cade does not recognize.

Cade flashes a smile and says, "So, we finally caught a break in the Maisy case? That's great news!"

His excitement crashes into a wall of silence.

Pointing to the third man, Whalen says, "Cade, I want you to meet special agent Bowlin. The T.B.I. has assigned him to this case."

Cade offers his hand to the unsmiling agent who returns the gesture and they shake.

Whalen nods toward a chair between agent Bowlin and Sheriff Harris. "Sit down Cade."

As Cade moves to the chair, Whalen turns his back to the room and looks out the window through the blinds. The ticking of the ancient clock on the wall fills the room.

"Why the somber mood?" Cade asks. "I figured I'd find everyone excited."

Turning from the window, Whalen sits in the chair behind his desk and says, "Remember that handprint on the wall at Maisy's apartment?"

"Sure," Cade replies. He feels his stomach twist.

"The T.B.I. got a definite match," Whalen continues. "Remember that trouble you had a while back for having a trunk load of marijuana? You were booked and fingerprinted. I'd forgotten all about it until I got a call from agent Bowlin. The handprint in Maisy's apartment is yours."

In spite of his calm demeanor, Cade's face reddens. He snickers and says, "Well yeah, I've seen Maisy. But, my gosh, what man around here hasn't?"

Sheriff Harris looks at him. His eyes darken and his expression is grim. Through clenched teeth he says, "I ain't."

Cade looks from the sheriff to Whalen to agent Bowlin. "Whoa here fellas. Are you thinking I killed Maisy? Because if you are, you're crazy. Why would I want to kill her?"

Agent Bowlin crosses his legs and says, "That crime scene was wiped down by someone who knew what they were doing. In spite of all the traffic that the sheriff tells me probably went through that apartment, there was only one print found that wasn't the victim's. That was yours."

"How do you explain that?" Whalen adds.

"And why," the sheriff asks, "would there be a full hand print on a wall? I'll bet you couldn't find a full handprint of mine on any wall in my house."

Looking at the sheriff, Cade says, "I really can't explain that. And unless I'm being charged, I don't believe I have to. What I do in my private life is my business."

"How often did you see Maisy?" Whalen asks.

"Before I answer that question, do I need to consult a lawyer?"

Whalen looks to agent Bowlin. "Mr. McDade," the agent begins, "we are not in a position to make any charges at this time. We are still gathering information. If you would like to help us in that process, it would certainly be appreciated."

"And," the sheriff chimes in, "we might be able to keep in this room the fact that you've been screwing around on your wife."

Cade glances at the ceiling and then back at Whalen. "I had a thing with Maisy several years ago and we saw each other pretty regularly. But I probably haven't seen her in at least two years."

The other three men exchange glances.

Sheriff Harris says, "Agent Bowlin, is it possible for a print to stay that long?"

"There's no valid test for proving how long a print has existed.

I have no way to prove it was made last week or two years ago."

~~~~~~~~~~~~~~~~

Chapter Twenty-one

Ella and Tucker ride in silence in the front seat of Ella's small Ford Pinto. In the back seat Smiley Carter's knees stick up higher than the back of the front seat. The low roof forces him to sit bent over, placing his chin within inches of his knees. His bulk makes it impossible for Ella to see out her rear view mirror.

"I hope you all knows what you're doin'," Carter says.

Staring straight ahead, Tucker says, "Miss Ella says it's the only way an' that's good 'nuff fer me."

"You both know," Ella says, "that we cannot keep this information to ourselves. The authorities have to know. And I think Sheriff Ron Harris is the best place to start. I believe him to be an honest man."

"I s'pose," Carter says. "But what about that boat I stole? What's he gonna say about that? Smiley Carter's too old to be going to jail."

"This ain't 'bout you," Tucker snaps. "It's 'bout m' girl Maisy. You're just like all men. Y' think th' sun sets an' rises cause o' you." Her voice rises. "God forbid that anything bad happen t' you. While m' girl was killed an' dumped like an' animal into that nasty backwater in the bottom. Jesus!"

Carter's head drops a notch lower.

Ella uses her left hand to swipe tears off her cheeks. The movement catches Tucker's eye. Turning to look, she sees that Carter wasn't the only person stung by her words.

In a softer tone, Tucker says, "Ella, I didn' mean no harm."

"I know," Ella responds. "You only spoke the truth. That's the trouble with the truth sometimes. It may set you free, but first it will make you miserable."

Nodding his bowed head, Carter says softly, "That's so."

Turning on her blinker, Ella says, "Well, here we are. We'll soon know if this was the right thing to do."

The little car leans first to its left and then to its right as Tucker and Carter exit on opposite sides. The three of them stand beside the car as if they were waiting for a valet.

Suddenly the door of the Sheriff's Department opens and deputy Jessie Wilson appears. Pulling at his sagging pants, he says, "Ya'll come on in. Sheriff Harris is expecting you."

Ella leads the parade, followed by Tucker. As Carter passes Jessie, Jessie sticks out his hand, "Hey Smiley. How you been?"

Carter shakes the deputy's hand and says, "Doin' alright, I guess. When in the world is you gonna retire?"

Stepping in front to lead them to the sheriff's office, Jessie smiles and says, "They wouldn't know how to run this county without me."

Pausing at a closed door, Jessie knocks twice and opens the door. "You're company's here Sheriff."

From inside the room, Sheriff Harris's voice carries, "Bring them in."

As they enter the room the sheriff nods at each one and calls them by name. Motioning toward three chairs lined up in front of his desk, he says, "Ya'll have a seat."

"If ya'll don't care," he adds, "I'd like Jessie to stay. Sometimes it's better to have two sets of ears."

Ella looks at Tucker.

"Jessie ain't never don't nothin' t' me," Tucker says. "Let 'im stay."

Ella then looks at Carter who shifts in his chair.

Glancing from the sheriff to Jessie, Carter wipes his large

hand across his brow. Letting out a big breath, he says, "Okay."
Pointing to the office door, he adds, "But shut that door."

Sheriff Harris nods at Jessie who closes the door and sits in a
chair behind the three guests.

Turning his attention to the three, the sheriff says, "Before we
start let me say something." Handing a key toward Tucker, he
says, "We're all through with Maisy's apartment. You're free to
get her things whenever you want to."

After Tucker takes the key, he says, "Okay, this is your all's
show. What's on your mind?"

"Ron," Ella begins, "this might have something to do with
Maisy. Or it might not. Smiley Carter saw something back in
February that he just told me and Tucker about recently. I think
you need to hear his story."

Sheriff Harris raises his eyebrows and turns his attention to
Carter.

Licking his dry lips, Smiley Carter says, "Well here's what
happened…"

When Carter finishes his story, Sheriff Harris's mouth is
agape. He glances at his deputy who mirrors his shocked
expression. He opens and closes several desk drawers until he
produces a mashed cigarette package. Fishing out a bent cigarette,
he places it in his mouth and lights it.

Blowing smoke out his nose, he says, "Why in the hell haven't
you said something before now?"

Ella clears her throat. "Well Ron, there's a small issue that
might cause a problem for Smiley Carter. That's why he was so
reluctant. It's the matter of the boat."

Looking blank, the sheriff says, "The boat?"

"It's that Reelfoot boat," Carter says. "It's at my house in the shed."

"Are you telling me it was your boat that was used?" the sheriff asks.

Eyes widening, Carter says, "No! No sir! What I'm sayin' is that he drove off and left it at the river. I waited a couple of hours and he never come back. So – "

Understanding dawning, the sheriff says, "You took it."

"I took it," Carter says and drops his head.

Closing his eyes, the sheriff rubs his temples. "Okay, okay," he says without opening his eyes. "We'll get to that later." Looking at Carter, he says, "We need to pin down the exact night this happened. Can you do that?"

Carter raises his head and says, "The exact date?"

"Yes!" the sheriff explodes. "I need a date that the murder took place. I can't piece this puzzle together until I have a starting place."

"Well," Carter begins, "I know it was in February." Looking at Tucker, he says, "It was a week or so after we worked up your garden." Suddenly he smiles, "I remember! It was February 15. I thought it might be a good luck sort of thing to go fishing the day after Valentine's. Yes sir, it was February 15."

Sheriff Harris glances at his deputy in the back of the room and then looks at Carter. "Are you positive?"

"Yep, no doubt," Carter replies.

Standing up, the sheriff says, "That's all I need from you all right now. I really appreciate you coming in and telling me about all this."

"What'r y' gonna do now?" Tucker asks.

"We've got to check some things out," the sheriff answers. "Just let us do our job. We'll be in touch."

Deputy Wilson coughs and opens the office door. The three visitors stand and begin filing out. As Tucker is about to step through the door, the sheriff says, "Tucker, can I speak to you privately for just a second?"

Tucker turns to face the sheriff and steps back inside his office.

"Shut the door Jessie," he says. "But I want you to stay in here for this."

Once the door is shut, the sheriff asks, "You're familiar with the area where Maisy's body was found, aren't you?"

Folding her arms over her chest, Tucker blinks rapidly. "Might be. Might not."

Harris cocks his head to one side and says, "Let me put it this way. Some of our boys were in the bottom looking for clues to help us find Maisy's murderer. While searching through all that mud, they thought they found something important, maybe the remains of someone else's body that had been there a long, long time."

He pauses to let Tucker comment.

As if her features are set in stone, Tucker shows no emotion. The lock on her lips remains sealed.

The sheriff continues, "It turns out that what they found had nothing to do with Maisy. As a matter of fact, I'm not even sure what happened to the bones they found." Shifting his feet uncomfortably, he adds, "I guess I thought it was something you'd like to know. There's nothing left in those bottoms that has anything to do with Maisy or with you. Do you understand what I'm saying?"

Tucker looks from the sheriff to Jessie and back to the sheriff.

"Is that all ya'll got t' say?" she asks.

"One other thing," the sheriff says. "This week I learned of a saying my grandfather used to have. He said, 'Sometimes a person gets what's coming to them, even if it is outside the law.' I think my grandfather was right."

He motions at Jessie to open the door. When he does, Tucker strides past and heads to the waiting car outside.

Turning to the sheriff, Jessie gives a slight smile and says, "Good job sheriff. Your granddaddy would be proud of you."

"I hope so," the sheriff replies. "Now, you go pick up Cade McDade and bring here to my office. I'm going to find Whalen and fill him in. I don't care how you do it, but you keep Cade here until I come back with Whalen."

~~~~~~~~~~~~~~~~~~

Chapter Twenty-two

Sitting in Sheriff Harris' office, Cade McDade looks at Jessie. "What is this all about?"

Showing no emotion, Jessie says, "Can't say. I was told to find you, bring you here and keep you here until the sheriff gets back."

Cade crosses and re-crosses his legs. "Well this is ridiculous. I've got work I'm supposed to be doing for Whalen Kennedy, you know. Who's going to explain this to him?"

His question is met with a look of nonchalance by Jessie.

Suddenly the door to the office opens and Sheriff Harris strides in.

Immediately, Cade is on his feet. "I demand to know what the hell is going on here sheriff! Who's going to explain this to – " His voice trails off and his eyes widen as he sees Whalen enter the room.

Taking a more conciliatory tone, Cade extends his hand toward Whalen and says, "Am I glad to see you Whalen. I was beginning to feel like a hostage."

When Whalen does not shake his hand, he backs up a step. Looking from Whalen to the sheriff, he says, "Is this about Maisy?"

"What makes you say that?" the sheriff asks.

"The last time I had to meet with both of you, that was the topic de jour. So tell me, what is going on?"

"Let's all sit down," Whalen says.

Once they are seated, Whalen asks, "Do you own a Reelfoot boat Cade?"

Cade feels as if a sledge hammer has hit him in the chest. He laughs nervously. "A what?"

"You heard me," Whalen replies.

Licking his lips, Cade says, "Actually I do own a Reelfoot boat, but I haven't seen it in months. Someone must have stolen it."

"Jessie," the sheriff says, "have you had any reports made on a stolen Reelfoot boat?"

Speaking matter-of-factly, Jessie says, "Not to my knowledge sir."

With raised eyebrows, the sheriff looks at Cade.

"No, I didn't report it," Cade volunteers. "It was only worth a couple of hundred dollars. And I never used it that much anyway."

"When was the last time you used it?" Whalen asks.

Cade looks at Whalen and blinks. "Huh?"

"I want to know when was the last time you used your Reelfoot boat," Whalen says.

"Uh, I guess last fall or maybe in December," Cade says.

Whalen and the sheriff exchange a glance.

"Tell me this," the sheriff begins, "where were you the night of February fifteenth?"

Cade's head snaps toward the sheriff. "Huh?"

"Boy, have you got hearing problems?" the sheriff says. "February fifteenth. Where were you?"

Standing up, Cade says, "Look, I don't know what's going on. I feel like I'm being questioned like a suspect. Do I need to have a lawyer here? Am I being charged with something?"

"At this point," Whalen says, "we are simply looking for

answers to questions."

"Well maybe if you filled me in on what you are looking into, I might could be more helpful," Cade replies.

"I suppose that's fair enough," Whalen says. "Cade, we have a witness that places you in the Latham bottom on February fifteenth, near the site where Maisy Tucker's body was found."

Throwing his head back, Cade laughs loudly. "That is impossible! You are both crazy! Besides, why in the world would I kill Maisy? This feels like nothing more than a fishing expedition and I'm tired of it. Unless you are going to charge me with something, I'm leaving." He stands up.

"So," Whalen says, "if you were not in the bottoms on February fifteenth, can you tell us where you were?"

Cade jerks on his tie to loosen it. He walks to the door. Yanking it open, he turns to the men in the office and says, "If you must know, I was at my mother's house treating her with a Valentine's present." He slams the door behind him as he leaves.

Whalen looks at Sheriff Harris and Jessie. "What do you two think?"

"I believe he's lying," the sheriff says.

Nodding, Jessie says, "Absolutely. He started panicking when you told him about the eye witness."

"This is as twisted up as honeysuckle on a woven wire fence," Whalen says. "And he's using his mother as his alibi. So you believe Smiley Carter's story over Cade's?"

"Yes I do," the sheriff says. "Smiley's got no reason to lie, especially since he incriminated himself by admitting to stealing the boat. He could have told the story lots of ways and left that part out."

"But he didn't actually see what Cade got out of the trunk and placed in the boat, did he?"

"No, he didn't," the sheriff replies. "We need to get the T.B.I. boys back up here to go through the trunk of his car looking for evidence."

"We better get that boat as well," Jessie adds.

"Good idea," Whalen agrees. "But we'll need to go through another judge besides Judge Jack to obtain a search warrant."

"What's got me stumped," the sheriff says, "is why? What's his motive for killing her? She wasn't anything but a whore. You reckon she was going to tell his wife?"

Nodding, Whalen says, "Maybe, but if she did tell, it would be killing her own golden goose. Maybe when we get the coroner's report on the cause of death, it will give us some more clues."

"We should get that any day now, don't you think?" the sheriff asks.

"Why don't I give them a quick phone call," Whalen says. "They may have the results already and just waiting to type them up. Sometimes, if I can get through to the right person, they'll go ahead and tell me."

The sheriff turns the phone on his desk so that it faces Whalen. "Help yourself."

Picking up the receiver, Whalen dials the seven digit number from memory. There are a few moments of silence.

"Yes, this is Whalen Kennedy, district attorney. Is this Martha?....."

"I thought so. Listen, I need some help. You all have a body down there that I need a cause of death for – Maisy Tucker. I thought your people might have completed the autopsy and the report was just waiting to be typed up........."

"Sure, I'll hold..." He covers the mouthpiece and winks at Sheriff Harris.

In a moment he says, "Interesting. Thanks a bunch Martha. I'll take you out to eat at the Peabody sometime. Take care. Bye."

Placing the receiver in the cradle, he looks at the sheriff and says, "Maisy's body was full of this new street drug called Quaalude. Enough in her to possibly kill her. But that's not how she died. She died of drowning. Her lungs were full of water."

A low whistle comes from Jessie.

"So," the sheriff reasons, "the charge will definitely be murder, not just illegal disposing of a dead body, because he could have used that defense. You know, 'she overdosed, I panicked and dumped her body.'"

"Exactly," Whalen agrees. "But motive, that's the hitch pin in this case. If we can't find a motive, it's never going to fly past the grand jury."

~~~~~~~~~~~~~

Chapter Twenty-three

Ella stops at the four-way stop sign beside the court house. There is no traffic coming or waiting behind her, so there is no need to be in a hurry to move.

In the silence of the hesitation, Tucker says, "Will ya'll go with me t' Maisy's?"

"Now?" Ella asks.

"Now," Tucker says.

Peering at Smiley Carter in the rearview mirror, Ella's raises her eyebrows in an unasked question.

"Sure," he says. "I'll go with you two, if you wants."

Checking the traffic again, Ella says, "Then it's to Maisy's we go."

Unlocking the front door with the key Sheriff Harris gave her, Tucker cautiously opens it. The air inside hasn't moved since the electricity was disconnected months ago.

The three explorers stand inside, waiting for their eyes to adjust to the dimness.

Ella looks to Tucker for a cue on how she wants to proceed. When she sees Tucker assume her closed stance with arms folded across her chest, she says, "Do you know what you'd like to do or where you'd like to begin?"

When Tucker doesn't respond, Ella gestures at Carter, "Let's open the curtains and windows. That will let some light and some air in here."

Thankful to have something to do, Carter moves toward a window. "Yes ma'am. That's a good idea."

As fresh air and natural light begin drifting in, Tucker unfolds her arms from her chest. "I don't know what I'm supposed t' be doin'. I don't know th' person who used t' live here. She died t' me a long time ago. It's like I'm a burglar 'r somethin'."

Looking around the apartment, Ella says, "Maybe you will find some things here that you'd like to keep for yourself or to give to the children. What about her dishes and things? Would you like to have those?"

"I s'pose," Tucker says reluctantly, looking toward the kitchen. "Carter, why don'chu stack all of 'em on th' table. We'll git some boxes later n' take 'em t' th' house."

"Good idea," Carter says. He reaches into the cabinets and begins pulling out the plates.

"There might be some pretty hair things that April would like to have," Ella says.

"Go ahead," Tucker replies. "Help yoreself t' whatever y' find. You might like t' have some o' her fancy clothes, too."

Glancing down at her breast-less chest, Ella smiles wryly and says, "I don't think Maisy's clothes will fit me."

"Reckon yore right," Tucker agrees. She slowly walks from room to room while Ella and Carter go about their missions.

In a few minutes, Tucker calls out to them, "Y' know, there's one thing I'd like t' have. When she left home I give 'er th' only thing I ever had that b'longed to m' mother. It was a family Bible with fancy picture in it. If'n ya'll see it, let m' know."

His hands full of glasses, Carter calls back, "Will do."

"We'll both help you look for it," Ella adds, and waves Carter to join her.

For the next fifteen minutes, there is an intense search for the family Bible. Each newly found cubby hole turns out to be an empty promise.

They finally all assemble in the living room, hands on hips. They scan again, looking for any overlooked hiding places.

"I went through every book in that bookcase," Ella says, "but I didn't reach on the top of it. Could it be up there?"

Walking to the bookcase, Carter reaches to his full height and says, "Let ol' Smiley Carter see what he can find."

His hand pats across the top. Suddenly he stops and his eyes brighten. "I found something. It's big."

With a grunt, he grips and lifts the object he has found. Once it clears the edge of the bookcase, it is obvious it is the family Bible.

"Lordy!" Tucker exclaims.

"You found it," Ella cries out.

As Carter lowers it for all to see, an envelope escapes and flutters to the floor. All eyes follow its descent. In bold three inch letters are printed the words, FOR TUCKER.

Forgetting about the Bible, Ella and Carter watch Tucker as she slowly bends and picks up the envelope.

As if there was a need to clarify the clear inscription, Tucker reads aloud, "For Tucker."

Bending her head down a notch, Ella says, "There's something written on the back, too."

Tucker turns the envelope over and reads, "To be opened upon my death."

Ella gasps.

"Jesus Christ!" Carter says, and takes a step back.

"What's this mean?" Tucker asks no one in particular.

"Why didn't the investigators find this?" Ella asks.

Answering her own question, she surmises, "They just didn't think about looking way up there."

"What's this mean?" Tucker repeats her question while looking toward Ella.

Looking at her friend, Ella says, "Evidently Maisy wrote this before she died, sealed it up and intended it to be read by you only, just in case she died before you."

"This here's a bad sign," Carter says, concern edging his voice. Shaking his head, he adds, "I gots me a bad feeling about this."

"Let's just sit down for a minute," Ella says.

Carter chooses the loveseat, Ella an armchair, and Tucker the recliner. Everyone sits on the front edge of their resting place. Apprehension tinges the air.

Tucker slowly rotates the envelope in endless loops. Looking at the envelope on its circuitous route, Tucker says, "You mean m' Maisy thought someone was a'goin' t' kill 'er? That's why she done this 'ere letter?"

"That's what it sounds like to me," Ella answers. "Maybe the letter will give answers to everyone who is searching for explanations to Maisy's murder."

Handing the envelope toward Ella, Tucker says, "Here, you read it out loud. I can't do it. Besides, I ain't much of a reader."

Rows of furrows suddenly crease Ella's forehead. Shaking her head, she says, "Oh no Tucker. This is for you. It's written to you. It may be very personal. Please don't ask me to do this."

In a tone of voice only heard by April in quiet moments, Tucker says, "Ella, please, you have to do this for me."

As if she were reaching for a poison dart, Ella takes the envelope between her thumb and index finger. Holding it up toward the window, she spies the direction the letter lies inside.

She tears off the opposite end of the envelope and pulls out a sheet of paper.

~~~~~~~~~~~~~~~~~~~~~

Chapter Twenty-four

Ella slides the letter from its hiding place and lets the envelope fall to the floor. As she unfolds it, it is apparent that is hand written on yellow sheets of paper from a legal pad. At first glance, Ella is amazed at the beauty and style of the penmanship.

She finds no salutation as an opening. Clearing her throat, she begins reading:

Since you are reading this, it means it finally happened. I'm dead like you've wanted me to be since I was born. I hope you are happy now.

All I ever wanted from you was a kind word. I gave up trying to please you a long time ago.

Ella refolds the letter and says, "Tucker, I don't think I should be reading this. It is a very private letter."

"She ain't gonna say nothin' I ain't heerd afore," Tucker replies. "It ain't no skin off my nose if you hear it, too."

"Very well then," Ella says. Opening the letter, she continues reading.

I know you never have been proud of me and the way I've lived my life, but I did the best I could. At least I never lived off of welfare like you.

I will give you credit for taking care of my kids. I know they love me and that's all that matters to me. I was planning on getting all of them back real soon. But if you are reading this letter, then it looks like they are yours for good.

I think my kids deserve to know who their daddies are. I was going to tell them eventually, but now I guess that's up to you.

All three men would probably deny the child was their's, but I know what I know. There ain't no doubt.

August's daddy is Smiley Carter.

"What the - ?!" Carter bolts out of his chair.

Ella repeats her plea, "I am very uncomfortable reading this letter."

"Th' cork's done been popped now," Tucker says. "Ain't no sense in stopping. Sit down Carter."

Smiley Carter slowly sits back down, his eyes wide and reddening.

Ella returns her attention to the letter.

August's daddy is Smiley Carter. I was only with him one time. We had a few drinks together and one thing led to another. You know how it is. The thing I don't understand is that ever since he had sex with me, it's seemed like he hated me.

Carter mumbles something unintelligible. Ella glances at him, but continues reading.

March's daddy was with the carnival that came through town in June, the summer before March was born. I think his name was Scotty. He was really cute. He promised me he would take me with him when the carnival left town. But he skipped out on me and I never heard from him again. Well, that's his loss.

April's father was the only man I really loved. He took care of me like no one ever did. He made me feel alive and wanted. I always thought we would marry. His name is –

Ella's hand flies to her mouth. A muffled, "No," escapes through the closed door her hand tried to place on her mouth.

Slowly withdrawing her hand from her mouth, she begins reading in a whisper.

His name is Cade McDade. Yes, Judge Jack's son. Crazy, isn't it? The children of two people who hate each other end up screwing each other. I got a laugh out of it quite often.

But I guess if you're reading this, then the last laugh is yours.

I'll probably see you in hell.

Signed: The one and only – Amazing!

The silence that fills the room acts like a vacuum and removes all the air. The three visitors look shell shocked.

Ella's complexion turns as pasty as it was the day she moved into the McDaniel place beside Tucker.

Smiley Carter sags heavily into the loveseat, his eyes unfocused.

Her mouth agape, Tucker reaches to her face with a trembling hand and slowly removes her glasses.

Finally, Carter speaks. "It just don't seem possible. August is my boy."

His comment jerks Tucker and Ella out of their individual mental and emotional calisthenics that were triggered by the letter.

Ella notices Tucker's fists tightening and the flushness in her cheeks.

"Smiley Carter." Tucker spits his name out like a stream of her tobacco juice. "After all these years of bein' friends, you and Maisy…" Her voice trials off.

Tucker suddenly staggers to her feet and bolts toward Carter. "You sorry s.o.b.!" she bellows.

Carter's mouth and eyes open in shock at the approaching Tucker. He throws up his arms in self defense as she crashes into him. Tucker's momentum flips the love seat on its back, spilling Tucker and Carter on to the floor.

"Tucker!" Ella screams. She jumps up and races to where the two are grappling on the floor.

Tucker's hands are gripped around Carter's throat. He seizes her wrists and tries to pry her loose.

Grabbing Tucker's shirt, Ella yells, "Stop it Tucker! Stop! Get off of him and calm down."

Carter rolls in order to pin Tucker underneath him. The movement catches Ella's legs and she collapses like a felled tree into an end table. The lamp clatters to the floor and Ella cries out in pain.

Her sharp cry knifes its way through Tucker's adrenalin filled brain. Releasing her grip on Carter, she barks, "Git off'n me! Ella's hurt!"

Carter quickly obeys and they turn their attention to Ella who has pushed herself into a seated position.

Taking Ella's hand in his, Carter asks, "Miss Ella, are you alright?"

Tucker sits beside Ella and puts her arm around her shoulders. "I'm sorry Ella. I lost m' head. It's my fault. You okay?"

Rubbing her knee, Ella says, "Yes I'm okay. I just banged my knee on that coffee table. Help me up."

Carter and Tucker each grab an arm and help Ella to her feet. Carter slowly lifts the loveseat back in place. They return to their seats.

Reaching on the floor and picking up the letter, Tucker says, "Y' think we better show this t' th' sheriff?"

There is a pause as each of them considers the implications of such a move.

"I don't think we have a choice," Ella replies.

"Seems to me it's the only thing we can do," Carter agrees.

A look of astonishment spreads across Ella's face. "Do you know what I just realized? If what this letter says is true, April is my granddaughter, too."

DAVID JOHNSON

~~~~~~~~~~~~~~~~~

Chapter Twenty-five

Sitting in the leather chair in front of his father's desk, Cade McDade lifts the glass to his lips. He gulps the alcohol, hoping the burning effect will dull the power of the verbal tsunami that is about to inundate him.

Judge Jack McDade slams his open palm on the desk. The report sounds like a gunshot. His face is crimson.

Looking at Cade with disgust, Judge Jack roars, "Maisy Tucker! You and Maisy Tucker! I cannot believe my ears. You could have your choice of any woman in the county and you choose a low class, two-bit whore. Someone who's spread her legs more times than I've spread mustard on a sandwich.

"What in the world were you thinking about?! No, don't answer that question. It's pretty obvious what you were thinking about."

The Judge pauses to pour himself another drink. After swigging it down, he wipes his lips with the back of his hand. Without warning he hurls the empty glass in Cade's direction. "You fool!"

Cade freezes in shock. The glass sails over his head, missing him by inches, and shatters against the wall behind him.

Getting up from his chair, Cade says, "Good god dad, calm down. Are you trying to kill me?"

"That's not a bad idea," Judge Jack snaps. "You know, something else I don't understand is why you decided to kill her just because she was going to tell your wife you'd been sleeping with her. I'm confident Julie knows all about your indiscretions. But she's too enamored with her comfortable life to kick you out."

Cade's face reddens. He avoids eye contact with his dad. "I guess I just got nervous. Maisy had a vicious mouth. I didn't know how much trouble she might stir up. And I was afraid Whalen might fire me, if he heard about it."

Cautiously being seated again, Cade continues, "There's no way they can pin this on me. All they have is one handprint on a wall in her apartment. But I get this feeling that Whalen and the sheriff are dead set on accusing me of the murder."

The Judge runs his hands through his hair. "Alright, so let me be sure I've got this straight. Maisy actually died of an overdose on the drug Quaalude. Right?"

"Exactly," Cade replies. "I put enough in her drink to knock out an elephant. It should look like she died at her own hands."

"Okay," the Judge says, "but what about Smiley Carter's statement about seeing you in the bottoms with a boat and something bundled up?"

A derisive laugh erupts from Cade. "The word of a nigger about something he saw at night time? We both know that will never stand up under vigorous cross-examination."

Judge Jack's expression does not mirror Cade's sudden light heartedness. "What you don't know," the Judge says, "is that Smiley Carter was a highly decorated veteran in World War Two. He was a sniper. Everyone knows his eyesight is keener than anyone's around."

The smile slides off of Cade's face like melting wax down the side of a candle. "Oh," he says weakly.

He eases to the edge of his seat and, placing his fists on his father's desk, says, "All we have to do is go see mother and convince her to give me an alibi for February fifteenth. I'm sure they will go see her. Once she backs up my alibi, that'll end their witch hunt."

"And even if she doesn't," the judge muses, "they don't have a motive for the murder, do they? Is there anything else you're not telling me?"

Pouring another drink, Cade replies, "Absolutely not. They can fish all day and they won't find a motive for me murdering

Maisy."

"Nonetheless," the judge says, "we need to have all bases covered. We'll go see your mother first thing in the morning. I'll pick you up at eight."

Sitting in Shorty's Diner, Whalen Kennedy listens intently as Sheriff Ron Harris tells him about the letter to Tucker that was found in Maisy's apartment.

Incredulous, Whalen asks, "You've seen the letter yourself?"

"With my own two eyes," the sheriff replies. "Tucker and Ella brought it to the jail. First of all I couldn't believe we or the T.B.I. had not found it during our search of Maisy's apartment. We turned that place upside down. And when I read the letter I felt like an explosion took place in my head."

"How many more twists is this case going to have?" Whalen asks.

"I know what you mean," the sheriff says. "Think about it, one of Tucker's grandchildren is also the grandchild of Judge Jack McDade. I don't know what word to use to describe that."

"Our old high school English teacher, Miss Perry, would say it is a perfect example of irony," Whalen says. "Where is the letter now?"

"I locked it up in the safe in my office, just to be safe."

Deep in thought with the implications of this new evidence, they fall silent while diving into their hamburgers and drinks.

Breaking the silence, Whalen says, "This certainly explains all the magazine articles we found in Maisy's apartment on DNA testing and paternity tests. Especially that most recent one on HLA typing ."

"HLA typing? What's that?" Sheriff Harris asks.

"It's the latest test for proving paternity. It's actually very accurate and is even admissible in court. The first of its kind."

The sheriff whistles, "I'll bet you anything that she threatened him with a paternity suit."

Nodding agreement, Whalen says, "I'd say we've discovered our motive for murder."

"But what about his alibi for the night of February fifteenth? How could he have been out at Ella McDade's and be in the bottoms at the same time?"

Whalen's expression saddens. "I forgot about that. But if he lied to us about everything else, could he be lying about that, too?"

Nodding, the sheriff says, "Sure he could. But he would have to know that we would check out his alibi."

"Unless," Whalen suggests, "he panicked and made up his alibi on the spot, right when we questioned him."

"Which means he'll be heading out to his mother's very shortly to talk her into helping him," the sheriff surmises.

Pulling back the cuff of his shirt to look at his watch, Whalen says, "Wow, it's nearly ten o'clock. I don't want to go out there and wake her up. Let's go in the morning. I'll pick you up at nine."

"I'll be waiting," the sheriff replies.

Chapter Twenty-six

Placing the last rinsed plate in the dish drainer, Ella McDade cocks her head to one side at the sound of a car door closing. She pulls the drain plug in the sink to let the dirty dish water run out and wipes her hands on her apron. Turning, she walks to the front window to peer out and see who her visitor might be.

Before she arrives at the window, there is a polite knock on the front door. Opening it, she sees her son, Cade, smiling broadly.

"Hello mother," he says. Taking a step in her direction, he says, "Can we come in?"

A frown slaps itself on her face, chasing away the relaxed expression that had been there only moments before. The "we" has triggered her adrenal system. Every fiber in her body is on alert.

Not waiting for her to respond to the question, Cade and Judge Jack walk past her.

She recognizes Judge Jack's furrowed brow to be a sign of concern that stands in direct contrast to Cade's light hearted air.

After she shuts the door and turns to face them, Cade embraces her and kisses her forehead.

"How have you been mother? I've been so busy with the family I haven't been out to see you like I should have. But you look great!" Moving to the couch, he says, "Can we sit down?"

Casting a wary eye toward Judge Jack, Ella joins Cade on the couch, while Judge Jack sits in an arm chair across from them.

"So what's wrong?" Ella asks.

"Wrong?" Cade says. A wounded expression replaces his smile. "Why do you ask that? Can't a son come visit his mother without there being something wrong?"

"Of course he can," Ella replies coolly, "but not my son. My son comes by when he's in trouble and when he wants something."

Cade is unable to withstand her piercing, unflinching gaze. He turns to his father with a pleading look.

Unexpectedly, Ella grabs Cade's chin between her thumb and fingers. Jerking his head to face her, she says, "Look at **me**. **You** came to see **me**. For once in your life, be a man and quit expecting others to bail you out."

Seeing the color in Ella's cheeks, Judge Jack says gently, "Now Ella – "

Extending her other arm in Judge Jack's direction, with her open palm toward him, she says curtly, "And **you** stay out of this."

Relinquishing her hold on Cade, she says, "Now, tell me why you are here."

"Honestly," Cade begins, "there is no real trouble. It's more like imagined trouble. It's about what someone thinks I did. The sheriff and Whalen have it in their head that I had something to do with Maisy's murder."

Feigning surprise, Ella says, "You and Maisy? Why would anyone think that you ever had anything to do with that woman? Everyone knows her reputation and that it is well deserved."

Hanging his head, Cade replies, "Uh, well you are right about that, but I have to be honest and admit that I was involved with Maisy some time ago for a very brief time."

Slowly turning her head toward Judge Jack, Ella says in an icy tone, "Well the apple surely doesn't fall far from the tree in this family, does it? You boys just can't seem to keep your pants zipped up, can you?"

"Now look Ella," Judge Jack says, "there's no use in talking like that."

Ella's eyes throw a dagger toward Judge Jack that seems to

immobilize him. "Really?" she asks. "There's no need in telling the truth? Is that what bothers you Jack? Listening to the truth and hearing what kind of example you've set for your son?"

Seeing his father's jaw muscles flexing in anger, Cade attempts to defuse things by saying, "Let me tell you what's going on mother. The T.B.I. found my handprint in Maisy's apartment. But that only tells that I was there at some point in time. It can't be dated. That's what made them turn their attention to me in the first place.

"But what really set them on trail is a concocted story by Smiley Carter. He told them that he saw me in the bottoms one night in February while he was night fishing. He said I put something in a boat and went up the river. When I returned, supposedly there was nothing in the boat. He said he could positively identify me as the person he saw.

"Can you hear how this is all a bunch of conjectures?"

"That's an interesting story," Ella replies. "But why in the world would you supposedly want to murder Maisy?"

"Exactly!" Cade responds. "There is no motive. That's where it all falls apart."

Clearing his throat, Judge Jack looks at Ella and asks, "May I say something?"

"Certainly," she says.

"What really brings us here," he begins, "is that in his statement Smiley Carter gives a specific date that he saw Cade and thereby a specific date for when the murder might have taken place."

Eyes widening, Ella says, "Oh really? What date is it?"

"February fifteenth," Cade answers.

An uneasy silence falls on the group. Ella sees that both men are looking at her expectantly. She looks from one to the other, trying to discern their hidden motives.

"Well?" she says.

"Well what?" Cade replies.

"Well, where were you on February fifteenth? Tell them where you were and that will clear all this up, won't it? If you weren't where he said you were and if you don't have a motive for murder, then that shuts down their investigation of you. Right?"

Cade blushes. "And that's where the problem is. You see, if I reveal where I was on the fifteenth, it's going to compromise someone else. And I really don't want to do that."

Ella laughs.

Both men look at her with expressions of shock.

"I don't think this is a laughing matter," Judge Jack says.

Regaining her composure, Ella says, "I'm laughing because both of you are laughable. You've come here to ask me to give you an alibi for that night. Am I right?"

Tearing up, Cade says, "I was hoping that I could count on you to help me. You're the only place I can turn."

Like a striking snake, Ella's hand slaps Cade. "Do not patronize me. Do not try to play me like one of your pitiful whores."

Judge Jack springs out of his chair and yells, "Now hold on just a minute. Who the hell do you think you are?"

Ella stands up and says, "I'm the woman who knows – "

The sudden sound of two car doors closing has the effect of closing Ella's mouth before she completes her thought.

Chapter Twenty-seven

The sound of the car doors has taken everyone's attention and sent it scurrying outside, wondering who the muffled voices belong to that are approaching the house.

Ella voices the question that's on everyone's tongue, "Who in the world could that be?"

As if the question releases a tension spring, there is a knock on the door. And though the knock is expected, everyone jumps.

Ella walks past Judge Jack to answer the door.

Grabbing her arm tightly, he jerks her around to face him. "Whoever it is, send them on their way. We've got business to settle here."

A muted cry of pain escapes from Ella as she wrenches free of him. Straightening her clothes, she makes it to the door and opens it.

His Stetson hat set squarely on his head and his face grim, Sheriff Ron Harris says, "Good morning Ella."

Backing up and opening the door wide, Ella says, "Please come in."

Surprised to be invited in before asking, the sheriff hesitates. "Are you sure now is a good time?"

A little laugh that borders on hysteria slips from Ella, "Oh Ron, this is a perfect time."

Seeing Whalen Kennedy behind the sheriff, she adds, "Hi Whalen. I didn't see you at first. Both of you, please come in."

Recognizing the sheriff's voice, Judge Jack positions himself beside Cade to face the two new visitors. "Hello sheriff. Hello Whalen," he greets them. "Surprised to see you two boys out this early."

The sheriff gives an imperceptible nod and says, "Morning Judge. Hello Cade."

With a relaxed manner, Whalen says, "And I'm not surprised to see you here Judge. Not at all. And good morning to you, too, Cade."

Moving past her newest guests, Ella says, "Let me get a couple of straight-back chairs from the kitchen so that everyone will have a place to sit."

Reluctantly taking his eyes off Cade, the sheriff says, "Let me help you Ella," and follows her.

Bringing two chairs back from the kitchen, the sheriff offers one to Whalen.

"Let's all have a seat," Whalen says.

Cade and Judge Jack sit on the couch. Whalen and the sheriff sit side by side facing the couch. Ella sits in an arm chair where she can easily see both sets of men.

Looking at Cade, Whalen asks, "Did we interrupt something? I thought I heard loud voices when we got out of the car."

Smiling, Cade replies, "Not a thing. This is just a family get together."

"Let's cut all the b.s.," Judge Jack says. "Why are you two out here?"

Before Whalen can answer, Ella speaks up. "This is my house. Who is here or who isn't here is no concern of yours. That's my business. Maybe I invited Whalen and Ron out for coffee this morning."

Judge Jack's cheeks turn crimson. His jaw juts out. "My apologies Ella. Of course, you are right."

A slight look of satisfaction flits across Ella's features. Looking toward Whalen and the Sheriff, she says, "So what brings you two out here on this pretty morning?"

"Originally," Whalen begins, "we wanted to ask you a few questions. But since Cade is here I think I'd like to ask him some questions."

"That's fine," Ella says. Turning to Cade she says, "I'm sure Cade wouldn't mind, would you?"

Looking defiant, Cade says, "I've got nothing to hide."

"That's encouraging," Whalen says. "How long ago did you first start seeing Maisy?"

"Huh?" Cade replies.

"It's a simple question," the sheriff chimes in.

Looking uncertain, Cade says, "I'm not sure. I'd have to think about it."

Crossing his legs and leaning back in his chair, Whalen says, "I'm in no hurry. We'll give you all the time you need."

Confusion creases the wrinkles around Judge Jack's eyes as he looks at Cade. "Just tell the man what he wants to know. What's your problem?"

Cade flinches at his father's bark. "Okay, okay. I'd say it was probably seven or so years ago."

The sheriff and Whalen look at each other.

"That would fit," the sheriff says.

"Fit what?" Judge Jack asks.

Uncrossing his legs and leaning forward in his chair, Whalen says, "You both know that the biggest concern in murder cases is motive. That's where we were stumped in Maisy's case. Why would someone murder her?

"And then out of the blue we got our first lucky break when

Smiley Carter revealed his story."

A brief, scoffing laugh escapes from Judge Jack. "You both know that that man's story will never stand up in court."

Ignoring the judge, Whalen keeps his eyes fastened on Cade. "And yesterday we got our second break. It gave us the motive we'd been looking for."

A pause as pregnant as a woman at full term holds everyone's attention hostage.

A thin sheen of sweat pops out on Cade's forehead and above his upper lip.

"It was the darndest thing," Whalen continues. "All our investigators missed it when they went through Maisy's apartment."

Pausing again, Whalen's eyes bore into Cade. "How many people know that Maisy's daughter, April, is your child?"

Cade slumps back into the couch, his face ashen.

Judge Jack's eyes bulge in disbelief. "What?!" he roars. Standing, he continues, "That's the most preposterous thing I've ever heard. You're just making things up now. I thought better of you Whalen."

Without warning, the front door explodes into the living room. Shards of glass fly across the room. Ripped from its hinges, the door lands heavily and slides into an armchair.

Holding her axe handle like a baseball bat, Tucker steps through the open doorway.

~~~~~~~~~~~~~~~~~~

Chapter Twenty-eight

Like a bull charging a matador, Tucker lumbers across the floor toward Judge Jack.

Jumping from her chair, Ella screams, "Tucker, no!"

Judge Jack's eyes fill with terror and he collapses on the couch beside his stricken son.

Sheriff Harris pushes past Whalen and steps in front of Tucker. "Halt right there Tucker," he says firmly.

Having her view of Judge Jack blocked by the sheriff, Tucker stops suddenly. Her eyes refocus on the sheriff.

When he sees he has her attention, he says calmly, "Everything is under control here. There's no need for any violence. Okay?"

Slowly lowering the axe handle, Tucker blinks rapidly. She looks at Ella. "You okay?"

Nodding, Ella says, "Yes, I'm fine."

Looking at the broken door, Tucker says, "I'm sorry. I can fix th' door fer y'. I heard shoutin' an' thought there was trouble."

Ella inhales deeply and says to Tucker, "Go get a chair from the kitchen and join us."

By the time Tucker has returned, the color has returned to both Cade and Judge Jack.

Scooting forward, Cade says, "Where in the world did you get the idea that April is my child?"

Waving the piece of paper, Whalen says, "In this letter that Maisy wrote. Tucker found it when she went to go through Maisy's things at the apartment yesterday. In it, she says very plainly that beyond a shadow of a doubt, you are April's father."

Waving his hand dismissively, Judge Jack says, "How do you know Tucker didn't write it herself and make up the story?"

"Because," Ella speaks up, "I was there when the letter was found."

Through clenched teeth, Judge Jack says to her, "You already knew about this? And didn't say anything to either of us? What kind of game are you trying to play?"

Deflecting the attention from Ella, Sheriff Harris interjects, "So Cade, if you started seeing Maisy around seven years ago that'd make April just about the right age, wouldn't it? When did she first tell you about April?"

"You don't have to answer that," Judge Jack cautions.

"That's true," Whalen agrees. "You don't have to answer anything. So far you haven't been charged with anything. However, I'm convinced we have the motive in hand."

Turning his chair to face Ella, he continues, "The only thing we have to establish is whether Cade has a legitimate alibi. He has told us that he was with you on the night of the murder, February fifteenth to be exact."

All eyes turn to Ella.

Judge Jack stands up and says, "Ella, may I talk to you in private for a moment?"

Tapping her axe handle on the wooden floor, Tucker says, "Th' onliest person you're gonna have a private talk with is me an' my axe handle. I've laid wood t' y' once before, an' I'll do it agin."

The Judge looks to the sheriff for help.

"Don't look at me," the sheriff says. "I've come between you once tonight, but I don't think I'll do it a second time. You're on your own. You just do what you think best."

The corners of Tucker's mouth turn up in a smile.

Sitting down, the Judge looks at Ella and says, "Then I'll say to you what I would have preferred to say in private. These men are about to charge your son and arrest him for murder in the first degree. If convicted, he could receive the death sentence.

"All you need to do is tell them the truth. Tell them that he came out here on the fifteenth to celebrate Valentine's Day with you, just like he told them he did. Nobody will doubt your word."

Holding his hands out toward her, he adds, "It's all up to you."

An electric silence falls on the room as everyone looks at Ella.

Ella bows her head and smoothes the wrinkles out of her apron. When she raises her head, there are tears in her eyes. Clearing her throat, she looks at Cade and says, "When you were a child, my world seemed perfect. The future was bright. I thought I had everything I wanted.

"But the older you got, the more you came under the influence and spell of your father. And that," she glances at Judge Jack, "proved to be your undoing. Your entitled attitude, narcissism, and manipulative ways have made you as dangerous a person as him." A tear slips from the cradle of her lower eyelid and rolls down her cheek. "And that saddens me.

"The double blow of getting cancer and being divorced felt like my personal tolling of the bell. When I moved out here, I thought my life was over. And when I learned my neighbor was the infamous Tucker, I decided life could get no worse. Death would have been a blessing."

Reaching her delicate hand toward Tucker's lap, she embraces Tucker's thick fingers and squeezes. She looks at each of her visitors. "Let me tell you all about this woman. I believe her to be the most incredible example of determination I have ever witnessed. She's rough and she's crude. And because of that she's judged harshly. But that's because no one knows all the incredible odds she's had to overcome."

The tears will not be held back any longer. They begin streaming down Ella's face. She looks at Tucker and sees her lip quivering. A solitary tear finds its way down Tucker's cheek and hangs tenaciously to her chin.

Turning back to the men listening, her voice rising, Ella says, "Tucker has become the truest friend I've ever had. Cade, you and your father expect me to turn my back on her and lie for you? The hell I will! For Tucker's sake, I will tell the truth."

She looks at Sheriff Harris and says, "Cade never came to my house on February 15. As a matter of truth, tonight's the first time I've seen him since Christmas."

Standing, she gives Cade a scathing look and says, "May God have mercy on your soul."

Taking his cue, the sheriff stands and says, "Cade McDade you are under arrest for the murder of Maisy Tucker."

As the sheriff reads Cade his rights, Ella feels a tug on her elbow. Turning, she sees Tucker, cheeks wet with tears, standing with her arms held open.

The two women embrace as Tucker says, "I love you Ella."

~~~~~~~~~~~~~~~~~~~~~

EPILOGUE

Sitting beside his lawyer in the stuffy courtroom, Cade McDade holds his breath as the jury enters the room and finds their seats.

When the judge enters, everyone stands. Once he is seated, everyone returns to their chairs. A murmur begins sweeping through the waiting audience.

The judge hammers his gavel and says, "Quiet!"

Reading through some papers in front of him, the judge keeps everyone in suspense a while longer. When he looks up, he asks, "Has the jury reached a verdict?"

A middle aged man wearing a white, open collared shirt and suspenders stands. "Yes sir your honor, we have."

Turning to Cade, the judge says, "Will the defendant please rise."

Cade pushes himself to a standing position.

Looking at the jury foreman, the judge asks, "What does the jury say?"

The foreman opens a folded piece of paper and reads, "We the jury find the defendant guilty of murder in the first degree."

The courtroom erupts in a cacophony of sounds.

The judge has to hammer his gavel several times before regaining control of the courtroom. He levels his gaze at Cade.

"Cade McDade, having been found guilty by a jury of your peers of the crime of murder in the first degree, I do hereby sentence you to the stiffest penalty at my disposal, that being death by the electric chair."

THE END

################

Don't miss Tucker's further adventures in the third book of the Tucker series - **<u>An Unexpected Frost</u>**. Tucker faces the biggest crises of her life. Her life skills are stretched to the breaking point. Will her ties to her new found friends, Ella and Smiley Carter, be enough to help her overcome?

Tucker's grandson disappears and the bank threatens to foreclose on her farm.

At the same time, Tucker's friend, Ella, is facing personal crises of her own. The tether that ties the hearts of these two women together is about to snap. Smiley Carter does his best to keep the friendships intact.

Living in the midst of these emotional storms is April who struggles to find solace and comfort. But the demons of regret and despair are beginning to haunt her dreams.

Tucker finds herself in a crisis of faith and asks the question, "Where is the person called God?!"

About the Author

David Johnson spent fifteen years as a Youth and Family Minister. He then went back to school and received a Master's Degree in Social Work from the University of Tennessee. For the past twenty years he has been a Marriage and Family Therapist.

He has had positions as the Clinical Director at the Christian Counseling Center of Western Kentucky; the Treatment Director at Spirit Lake Recovery; and is presently a counselor at the McKenzie Medical Center.

David is Licensed as a Marriage and Family Therapist and as a Master Social Worker.

He has conducted numerous marriage retreats and workshops. He's been interviewed on both radio and television.

David has been married for forty years and has two daughters and six grandchildren.

In his spare time he is the Director of the David Johnson Chorus.

Connect with David on

Twitter: #DavidJohnson_

Facebook

Or visit his blog: thefrontwindow.wordpress.com

Visit David Johnson's author page on Amazon to view other books by him:

- Real People, Real Problems

- Where is God when I Can't Find Him?

Made in the USA
Charleston, SC
15 June 2013